T0322204

EDOGAWA RAMPO

*Beast in the Shadows*

*Translated by Ian Hughes*

PENGUIN BOOKS

PENGUIN CLASSICS

UK | USA | Canada | Ireland | Australia
India | New Zealand | South Africa

Penguin Books is part of the Penguin Random House group of companies
whose addresses can be found at global.penguinrandomhouse.com.

Penguin
Random House
UK

This translation first published by Kurodahan Press 2006
This edition published 2023
007

Translation copyright © Ian Hughes, 2006
All rights reserved

Set in 11.25/14 pt Dante MT Std
Typeset by Jouve (UK), Milton Keynes
Printed and bound in Great Britain by Clays Ltd, Elcograf S.p.A.

The authorized representative in the EEA is Penguin Random House Ireland,
Morrison Chambers, 32 Nassau Street, Dublin D02 YH68

ISBN: 978-0-241-65691-4

www.greenpenguin.co.uk

*Beast in the Shadows*

It sometimes seems to me that there are two types of detective novelist. One, you could say, is the criminal sort, whose only interest is in the crime and who cannot be satisfied when writing a detective story of the deductive kind unless depicting the cruel psychology of the criminal. The other is the detective type, an author of very sound character whose only interest is in the intellectual process of detection and who is indifferent to the criminal's psychology.

Now the detective novelist I am going to write about, Ōe Shundei, belongs to the former category, while I fall into the latter.

Accordingly, while my business is concerned with crime, I am in no way a bad person, for my interest is in the scientific deduction of the sleuth. Indeed, it might even be apt to say there are few as virtuous as me.

The real mistake is that such a well-meaning person as me accidentally became involved in this case. Were I somewhat less virtuous, had I within me the slightest trait of evil, I could perhaps have come through without such regrets. I might not have sunk into this fearful pit of suspicion. Rather, I might now be living in the lap of luxury, blessed with a beautiful wife and great wealth.

Quite some time has passed since everything ended and while the awful suspicions may not have disappeared the raw reality is fading into the distance and becoming to some extent a thing of the past. Accordingly, I have decided to set this down as a kind of record and I think it could even be made into a very interesting novel, though even if I completed the work I would not have the courage to release it immediately. You see, the strange death of Oyamada that forms a crucial part of this record still lingers in people's memories and no matter how names were changed and disguising layers applied nobody would take it as simply a work of fiction.

Thus, there may well be people who could be bothered by this novel and I would be embarrassed and disturbed to discover this. To tell the truth, though, it is more that I am frightened. For not only was the incident itself strangely meaningless and as unfathomable as a dream in broad daylight, the fantasies I built up around it were so terrifying as to discomfort even myself.

Even now, when I think of it this world transforms into something peculiar. Rain clouds fill the blue sky, a sound as of drumming beats within my ear, and all darkens before my eyes.

Anyway, while I am not of a mind to publish this record right away, sometime, just once, I would like to use it to write one of the detective novels in which I specialize. These are simply what you might call the notes for it. Nothing more than a moderately detailed *aide-mémoire*. I intend to write much as if keeping a long diary in an old notebook, blank but for the section around New Year.

Before I describe the case, it would probably be useful to provide a detailed explanation of Ōe Shundei, the detective story author who is the protagonist in this case, of his style, and also of his somewhat unusual manner of life. While I had known him prior to the incident and had even engaged him in discussions in magazines, we had not had any exchanges at a personal level and I knew little of his daily life. I became somewhat more informed about this through a friend called Honda after the events took place. Accordingly, with regard to Shundei I think it most fit that I write about these things in the order in which they occurred and as it was the occasion that led to my becoming caught up in this strange case I will describe the facts I noted when I went to interview Honda.

It was in the autumn of last year, around mid October.

I had a notion to look at some old sculptures of Buddha so I went to the Imperial Museum in Ueno where I walked through the gloomy, cavernous rooms trying to muffle my footsteps. In the large deserted halls, the slightest sound echoed fearfully and I felt like suppressing not only my footsteps but also any impulse to clear my throat.

So deserted was the place, I could not help but ponder why it is that museums are so unpopular. The large glass plates of the display cabinets shone coldly and not a speck of dust had fallen on the linoleum. The building's high ceilings were reminiscent of a temple's main hall and the silence flowed back as if one were deep under water.

I was standing in front of a display case in one of the rooms gazing at an aged wooden bodhisattva that had a dreamlike eroticism. Hearing a muffled footfall behind me, I sensed someone approach with a light sound of swishing silk.

I was startled to see the reflection of a person in the glass in front of me. Projected over the bodhisattva was the image of a woman of class wearing a lined kimono of yellow silk and with her hair done in the *marumage* style denoting a married lady. She drew level with me and stared intently at the Buddhist form. I am embarrassed to admit that while pretending to look at the image I could not prevent myself from snatching occasional glances at her. That was how much she captivated me.

Her face was pale, but I had never seen such an attractive paleness. If mermaids exist, then I believe they must have charming skin like that of this woman. She had the oval face of the beauties of the past and every line, whether of her brows, nose, mouth, neck, or shoulder, had that feminine delicacy described by the writers of old that suggested she might disappear if touched. Even now I cannot forget her dreamlike, long-lashed eyes.

Oddly, I do not now recall which of us spoke first, but perhaps I created some pretext. A brief interchange about the objects in the display case formed a link, and after doing the rounds of the museum together we exited and chatted about many things. Our paths remained the same for a considerable time on the walk from Sannai down toward Yamashita.

As we spoke, the air of beauty she evoked deepened further. When she laughed there was something graceful and shy that produced a strange sensation in me as though I were gazing at an old oil painting of a saint or that reminded me of the mysterious smile of the Mona Lisa. When she laughed, the edges of her lips caught on her large, pure white eye teeth, creating a fascinating curve. A large beauty spot on the pale white skin of her right cheek set off that curve to create an ineffable expression at once gentle and nostalgic.

However, were it not for something odd I discovered on the nape of her neck, my heart would not have been attracted by her so powerfully and she would have seemed but a genteel and tender beauty likely to vanish if touched.

She concealed it with a skilful arrangement of her collar that betrayed no artifice, but as we passed through Sannai I caught a glimpse.

Visible on the nape of her neck was a swollen line like a red weal that looked as though it went deep down her back. While it seemed to be a birthmark, I also wondered whether it might not actually be a recent scar. The dark red weal wormed over the smooth white skin of her soft nape, and strangely the cruelty of it bestowed an erotic impression. When I saw it, the beauty that had seemed to me so dreamlike suddenly pressed in on me with a compelling sense of reality.

I learned that she was a partner in Roku-Roku Trading Company, that her name was Oyamada Shizuko, and that she was the wife of the entrepreneur Oyamada Rokurō. Fortunately, she was a reader of detective fiction and in particular an admirer of my works (I shall never forget how happy I was when I heard this), which meant that ours was the relationship of an author and a fan. As such, we could become better acquainted without a trace of unseemliness and I was spared an unwanted permanent parting of the ways. Following this, we began to exchange letters occasionally.

I was impressed with Shizuko's refined taste, for though a young woman she visited deserted museums. I was also pleased that she was a devotee of my detective fiction, often said to be the most intellectual in the genre. Thus, I fell for her completely, sending her meaningless letters on a frequent basis. For her part, she scrupulously replied to each one in a ladylike style. Imagine how happy it made this lonely bachelor to have made friends with such an admirable woman.

## 2

The epistolary exchange between Oyamada Shizuko and myself continued in this fashion for some months.

As our correspondence grew, I noted with considerable nervousness that my letters were undeniably, if unobtrusively, coming to contain a certain import, but it also seemed to me that the notes from Shizuko, while of the utmost propriety, were becoming infused with a feeling of warmth that went above what you would expect in a conventional exchange, though perhaps this was my imagination.

To speak plainly, I am embarrassed to say that I went to some pains to find out that Shizuko's husband, Oyamada Rokurō, was very much his wife's senior, that he looked older than his actual age, and that he was completely bald.

Then, around February this year, something strange began to surface in Shizuko's letters. I sensed that she was becoming very scared about something.

In one letter she wrote, 'recently something very worrying is happening and I find myself waking up in the night.'

The sentence was simple enough, but behind the words themselves the impression of a woman assailed by fear could be made out all too clearly.

'Sir, I wonder if you happen to be a friend of Ōe Shundei, who is also an author of detective fiction? If you have his address, would you let me know it?'

Of course, I knew Ōe Shundei's works very well, but I had no personal acquaintance with the man because he was extremely anti-social and had never attended any writers' gatherings. I had also heard a rumour that he had suddenly stopped writing around the middle of last year and had perhaps relocated but that his address was unknown. I replied thus to Shizuko, but when I thought that the fear she had recently been experiencing could be connected to Ōe Shundei I had an unpleasant feeling for reasons I shall explain later.

Shortly afterward, I received a postcard from her saying, 'I would like to ask your advice about a matter. Would you permit me to call on you?'

I dimly sensed the nature of this 'matter', but as I certainly did not imagine it would be particularly frightful I was aflutter with a foolish happiness and gave myself up to all manner of fancies regarding a pleasant second encounter.

On the same day Shizuko obtained my reply that I would be pleased to receive her, she visited my lodgings. So downcast was she when I met her in the entrance hall that all my hopes were dashed, while the 'matter' was extraordinary enough to extinguish the fancies I had entertained shortly before.

'I came here because I am really at a loss as to what to do. I thought that you would be kind enough to listen to me . . . but I'm not sure if perhaps it would not be too much of an imposition to speak so frankly when you still hardly know me.'

Shizuko laughed tenderly, highlighting her eye teeth and beauty spot, and then glanced up at me.

As the weather was cold, I had placed a rosewood brazier next to my work desk and she now sat down decorously on the other side of the oblong box with the fingers of both hands resting on its edge. Supple, fine, and graceful, but not overly thin, the fingers seemed to symbolize her whole body. Nor did their paleness reflect any ill health, for while their delicacy suggested that they might vanish if pressed they had an uncanny strength. And it was not just her fingers – this was precisely the impression she gave overall.

Perceiving her intensity, I too quickly became serious and replied, 'If there's anything I can do.'

'It really is the most awful thing,' she said, and leaning forward she reported the following strange events, mixed in with anecdotes from her own youth.

To simplify considerably what Shizuko then told me about herself, she came from Shizuoka and she had enjoyed the utmost good fortune up until she was about to graduate from the girls' school she attended.

The only thing approaching ill fortune that befell her was in her fourth year at the school when she was beguiled by the artifices of a youth called Hirata Ichirō and fell in love with him very briefly.

'Ill fortune' because this was only an eighteen-year-old girl playing at love as a result of the slightest impulse; she certainly did not love Hirata truly. However, even if she was not really in love, the other party was totally in earnest.

She found herself doing her utmost to avoid the relentless youth, but the more she did the stronger his resolve became. Eventually, a dark figure began to drift around outside the fence beside her home late at night and unpleasant threatening letters appeared in the post. The young girl trembled at the frightful reward for her youthful impulse. Her parents too were upset when they realised that she was not her usual self.

Just at that time her family suffered a serious stroke of bad luck, but it was actually favourable for Shizuko. As a result of the major economic upheavals then taking place, her father closed down his business, leaving behind debt so massive that makeshift solutions would not do. Much as if fleeing in the night, he was forced to rely on a slight acquaintance to hide away in Hikone.

Due to this unforeseen change in her circumstances, Shizuko had to withdraw from the girls' school just before she was due to graduate. Nevertheless, she felt relieved that the sudden relocation enabled her to escape from the obsessive attentions of the unpleasant Hirata Ichirō.

As a result of the situation, her father became ill and shortly after passed away, leaving the mother and daughter behind. For a while, they endured a miserable existence, but their misfortune did not continue long. Soon, Oyamada Rokurō, an entrepreneur from the same village where they were lying low, came into their lives. He was their rescuer.

Through glimpses from afar, Oyamada fell deeply in love with Shizuko and sought her hand through a go-between. For her part, Shizuko felt no dislike for Oyamada. Although over ten years older than her, he was smartly turned out in gentleman's attire and had a certain ambitious air about him. The marriage proposal discussions proceeded smoothly. Oyamada returned to his mansion in Tokyo accompanied by his bride Shizuko and her mother.

Seven years passed. Shizuko's mother died of an illness in the third year or so after their marriage and some time after that Oyamada travelled overseas for two years on important business (Shizuko explained that he had returned at the end of the year before last and that she had assuaged the loneliness of her solitary existence each day by attending classes to learn the tea ceremony, flower arrangement, and music). Excluding this, their household was relatively free of incident and the very harmonious relationship between the two was characterized by a succession of happy days.

Oyamada Rokurō was an extremely energetic man and over those seven years he increased his wealth through hard work. He also established a considerable reputation among his peers.

'I am truly ashamed to say that I was not truthful about the situation with Hirata Ichirō when I married Rokurō. Despite myself, I covered it up.'

Shame and sadness made Shizuko lower her long-lashed eyes, which filled with tears as she spoke in a pained low voice.

'It seems that he had heard about Ichiro somewhere and that he had some suspicions, but I assured Rokurō that I had not been with anyone but him, taking great pains to hide my relationship with Ichirō. I am still living this lie. The more suspicious my husband has grown, the more I have sought to cover it up. I think that no matter where they may be hidden, our misfortunes are truly fearful. Who would have thought that a lie told seven years ago, and that with not the slightest intention of ill will, should have been the seed for the suffering I now endure. You see, I had forgotten entirely about Hirata Ichirō. So much so that even when a letter from him suddenly arrived and I saw that the sender's name was "Hirata Ichirō", I was at a loss for a while to recall who he was.'

When she had finished, Shizuko showed me several letters from Hirata. She entrusted me with their safekeeping and I have them still. As it may assist in telling the story, let me here include the first of the letters:

*Shizuko. I have found you at last.*

*You did not notice, but I followed you from the place where I encountered you and so learned where you live. I also found out that your surname is now Oyamada.*

*You cannot have forgotten Hirata Ichirō. Surely you remember this miserable wretch.*

*A heartless woman like you cannot understand the agonies I endured after you abandoned me. How many times I wandered around your house late at night in anguish. But as my passion burned ever stronger, you grew cooler and cooler toward me. Evading me, frightened of me, you soon came to hate me.*

Can you fathom the feelings of a man who is hated after having been adored? Can you understand how my anguish turned to sobs, my sobs to hatred that hardened and took shape as a desire for revenge? When your family's situation so luckily enabled you to disappear from my sight without a word of farewell, as if fleeing, I passed several days sitting in the study without eating or drinking. And I promised to seek revenge.

Being young, I did not know how to find out where you had gone. Your father owed money to many people and he slipped out of sight without letting anyone know his whereabouts. I had no idea when I would see you again. But I remembered life is long and I could not believe that mine would end without ever once meeting you again.

I was poor and I had to work in order to eat. That was one reason preventing me from asking around about your whereabouts. First one year, then two, the days and months flew past like an arrow, but I had to maintain my struggle against poverty. I was preoccupied with finding my next meal.

Then, just three years ago I had a surprising piece of good luck. After failing at various occupations and reaching the depths of despair I decided to write a novel to dispel my gloom. This was a turning point, for I was then able to put food on the table by writing fiction.

As you are still a novel reader, I expect you may know a writer of detective fiction called Ōe Shundei. He has not written anything for a year, but I do not think his name will have been forgotten. Well, I am Ōe Shundei.

Perhaps you think that I have become preoccupied with my fame as a novelist and forgotten my hatred for you? No, no – it is precisely the deep hatred stored within my heart that has enabled me to write such gory novels. If my readers knew all that suspicion, tenacity, and cruelty were born from my vengeful heart, they would probably be unable to suppress a shudder at the evil presentiment lying within.

*So Shizuko, having secured a stable life, I sought you out to the extent made possible by time and money. Of course, I held no impossible hopes that I might recover your love. I have a wife, but one whom I wed in form only, to eliminate the inconveniences of life. In my mind, though, a lover and a wife are completely different things. You see I am not someone who forgets his hatred for a lover just because he has taken a wife.*

*Shizuko, now I have found you.*

*I am beside myself with happiness. The time has come for the prayers of many years to be answered. I have put together a means of wreaking my revenge on you with the same pleasure I have enjoyed for a long time in assembling the structure of my novels. I carefully considered the method whereby I might cause you the utmost suffering and fear and at last the moment has arrived to implement it. Just imagine my happiness! You cannot foil my plan by seeking protection from the police or anyone else. I have taken all sorts of precautions.*

*For the past year, the story that I have gone missing has circulated among journalists working for newspapers and magazines. Stemming from my misanthropy and preference for secrecy rather than anything directed at gaining revenge on you, this flight has been useful, unplanned though it was. And with even further subtlety I shall hide myself from the world and step-by-step I will push forward with my plan of revenge.*

*Of course, you must want to know what this plan is, but I cannot let the full outline be known right now because one of its effects is to gradually increase the fear as it unfolds.*

*Still, if you really want to hear, I wouldn't begrudge letting slip just a little piece of my revenge project. For example, I could recount for you in precise detail a variety of trivial little things that took place in your house four days ago, that is, on the night of 31 January.*

*From seven in the evening to half past seven, you were leaning on a small desk in the room you use for sleeping, reading fiction. The* book was 'Hemeden,' a collection of short stories by Hirotsu Ryūrō. The only story you read right through was 'Hemeden.'

You then asked the maid to serve some tea and from half past seven to seven forty you ate two *monaka* cakes from Fūgetsu and drank three cups of tea.

You went to the lavatory at seven forty five and about five minutes later you came back to the room. From then until ten past nine, you were lost in thought as you passed the time knitting.

Your husband came home at ten past nine. From around nine twenty until a little after ten you chatted with him, keeping him company while he enjoyed a drink. At your husband's suggestion, you took half a glass of wine. The bottle had just been opened and you used your fingers to pick out a tiny piece of cork that had entered the glass. Soon after finishing your drinks, you asked the maid to prepare your beds and once the pair of you had visited the toilet you got into bed.

Neither of you slept until eleven o'clock. When you again lay down in your bed the pendulum clock you had received from your parents struck eleven.

I expect you cannot suppress a feeling of fear at reading this faithful record, as precise as a railway timetable.

> From the vengeance seeker (this night of 3 February)
> to she who stole the love of my life

'I had heard the name Ōe Shundei before, but had not the slightest inkling it was the pen-name of Hirata Ichirō,' Shizuko explained uneasily.

Indeed, even among authors, very few knew the real identity of Ōe Shundei. Such was Hirata's antipathy to people and his aversion to being seen in society that I would probably never have heard his name had I not heard a rumour about his actual identity from Honda, who often came to my place and who had seen the copyright information.

There were three more threatening letters from Hirata, but the differences between them were slight (each bore the seal of a different post office). They all contained a promise to seek revenge, followed by a meticulous and accurate account of Shizuko's activities on a given night, with the times for these included. In particular, the secrets of her bedroom were outlined with painful frankness, down to the crudest detail. Acts and words that might cause one to blush were recounted with cold cruelty.

I could imagine what embarrassment and suffering she would have felt at showing those letters to another person, but I must say that it was a good thing that she resisted doing so until selecting me as her confidant. On the one hand, this indicated just how frightened she was that her husband should learn the secret of her past, namely that she had not been a virgin when she married, while on the other hand it underscored the strength of her trust in me.

'Apart from my husband's family, I have no close relations and there is no one among my friends with whom I am so intimate that I could talk about this, so while I realize it is an imposition I decided to ask you if you would be so kind as to advise me what I should do.'

On hearing this, my heart raced with happiness to think this beautiful woman was relying on me to such an extent. Of course, there were reasons why she would select me as her confidant, for like Ōe Shundei I was an author of detective fiction and I was an accomplished exponent of deductive reasoning, at least in my fiction. Notwithstanding this, she would not have asked me for my advice on such a matter unless she felt considerable trust and affection toward me.

Naturally, I accepted her request and agreed to help her as much as I could.

It seemed to me that for Ōe Shundei to have ascertained

Shizuko's movements in such detail, he must have either sub-
orned one of the servants in the Oyamada household, stealthily
entered the household and concealed himself close to Shizuko,
or carried out some similar nefarious plot. Based on Shundei's
style, I deduced that he was just the sort of chap to go to such
weird lengths.

I asked Shizuko if she had noticed anything like this, but
strangely it seemed there was not the slightest trace. The servants were all trustworthy staff who had lived with the family
for many years, while the house's gateway and fences were very
secure because her husband was unusually nervous. Accordingly even if someone were able to sneak into the house, it
would be almost impossible to approach Shizuko in her room,
within the recesses of the building, without catching the eye of
one of the servants.

However, the truth is that I was scornful of Ōe Shundei's
ability to carry out such an action. What could a mere detective
novel writer do? At most, he could use his craft to write letters
to frighten Shizuko, but I convinced myself that he would be
unable to go beyond that and implement an evil scheme.

While it did seem somewhat strange that he had ascertained
Shizuko's movements in detail, this too appeared to be a ploy
based on a sleight of hand common to his trade and I simply
supposed that he had obtained the information from someone
without going to any great trouble himself. To assuage Shizuko's concerns, I gave her my understanding of the situation and
as it would also be advantageous to me, before sending her
home I assured her that I would determine Ōe Shundei's whereabouts and if possible convince him to put an end to this
nonsense.

I focused on calming Shizuko down rather than examining
various points in the threatening letters from Shundei. When
we parted, I said to her, 'I think it would be best if you didn't say

anything about this to your husband. This is not so serious an incident as to require you to expose your secret.'

Fool that I am, I wanted to continue for as long as possible the pleasure of talking alone with her about a secret that not even her husband knew.

Nevertheless, I did indeed intend to establish the whereabouts of Ōe Shundei. He was completely opposite to me in terms of character and I disliked him intensely. I couldn't stand the crone-like stream of suspicion-filled whining or that air of self-importance fed by the clamour of his degenerate readers. So I thought that if things turned out well, I would like to reveal his underhand acts and expose his tear-reddened, humiliated face for all to see. But I did not envisage how difficult it would be to ascertain the whereabouts of Ōe Shundei.

3

As noted in his own letter, Ōe Shundei was a detective story writer who had emerged quite suddenly some four years ago after having pursued a number of occupations for which he was unsuited.

At that time there was hardly any detective fiction written by a Japanese author and accordingly when he released his first work the reading public greeted the rarity with great acclaim. If you were to couch it in hyperbole, you could say that he instantly became the darling of book-reading society.

Although he was not particularly prolific, a string of new works were released by a variety of newspapers and magazines. Gory, guileful, and evil, every one of these works was full of unpleasant expressions that caused your hair to stand on end, but that actually became a feature that attracted readers and his popularity continued unabated.

At about this time, I changed from writing books aimed at younger readers to detective fiction, and my name became relatively well known in the detective novel market, where there were few practitioners. However, my style was so different from Ōe Shundei's as to be almost entirely opposite.

In contrast to his gloomy, sickly, and grotesque approach, my style was bright and reflected ordinary values. In the natural flow of events, our works often competed and there were even times when we disparaged each other's fiction. Infuriatingly, though, it was usually I who scorned Shundei's writings, for while he occasionally disputed my contentions, for the most part he maintained an aloof silence. And he released his shocking stories one after another.

While I disparaged his works, I could not help but notice in them a certain eeriness. He had a passion that burned like an unquenchable ghostly flame and this unfathomable appeal captured his readers. If this stemmed from his bitterness toward Shizuko, as his letter suggested, then one could half nod in assent.

If the truth be told, I felt unspeakable jealousy each time one of his works received acclaim. I even harboured a childish perception of him as my enemy. Oh, that I could beat him! The desire rankled endlessly within my soul.

But just one year ago, he suddenly stopped writing novels and went to ground. It was not as if his popularity had waned, and the magazine hacks searched high and low for him, but for some reason he was not to be found. While I disliked him, I became a little sad when he suddenly disappeared. I had that lingering, childish feeling of emptiness one has when a 'favourite' enemy has gone.

Now I had heard news of Ōe Shundei from Oyamada Shizuko and what strange news it was. I am ashamed to say that I was secretly happy to have met my old rival again, albeit in such strange circumstances.

But was it not a natural progression, I thought, for Shundei to divert the imagination he had focused on constructing his detective tales into carrying out a plan of action?

I am sure many people are aware of this, but he was the kind of man you would call a 'fantasist about the criminal life.' In the gory pages of his manuscripts, he lived a criminal life with the same passion a brutal killer feels when he commits murder.

I am sure his readers will recall the strange ghastliness pervading his novels. They will remember the uncommon suspicions, secrecy, and cruelty that consistently filled the pages of his works. We can catch a glimpse of this in the following weird lines from one of his novels.

'Perhaps the time would come when he would not be content with just writing novels. Bored with the vanity and monotony of life, he had at least found pleasure in expressing his unusual imagination by putting words on paper. That was the impulse for him to begin writing fiction. But now he had even become bored with the novels. Where would he find the stimulation he craved now? Crime, yes, there was only crime left. Having exhausted so many other avenues, only crime's frisson remained.'

The author was also very eccentric in his ordinary life. Shundei's misanthropy and secrecy became known among other writers and magazine journalists. It was very rare for a visitor to be shown through to his study. His seniors in social standing were turned away at the door with equanimity regardless of their rank. He also moved house often and never attended writers' gatherings on the pretext of illnesses that lasted more or less all year.

Rumour had it that he lay all day and night in a bed that was never made up, doing everything, whether eating or writing, from a recumbent position. Apparently he closed the window shutters in the day, writhing in the candle-lit gloom of his room as he penned those eerie reveries of his.

When I was told that he had stopped writing novels and disappeared, I secretly imagined that he had perhaps set up a base in the jumbled back streets of Asakusa and begun to put his fantasies into action, much as he often described in his fiction. Would he be able to carry it out? Not six months had passed when he appeared before me as someone who did indeed intend to put his fantasies into action.

It seemed to me that the quickest way to ascertain Shundei's whereabouts would be to ask around in the arts sections of the newspapers or to talk to the magazine journalists. Nevertheless, such was the extreme eccentricity of Shundei's daily life that he only received visitors infrequently. In addition, as the magazine houses had already tracked him down before, I needed a journalist who was on very intimate terms with him. Fortunately, a magazine editor with whom I was friendly was just the right person.

A scribe who worked out on the streets, Honda had an outstanding reputation as a specialist in his field. There had been a time when his task was to get Shundei to write fiction, much as if Shundei was Honda's main assignment. In addition, in keeping with his role as a journalist working the front line, Honda had considerable investigative skills.

Accordingly, I telephoned him and invited him over. First I asked him to tell me about Shundei's day-to-day life, of which I knew little.

He replied very informally.

'Shundei, you say? Oh, he's a boor, isn't he?'

He looked like Daikoku, the stout god of wealth, as he smiled sardonically, before answering all my questions earnestly.

According to Honda, Shundei had been living in a rented house in Ikebukuro when he began to write novels, but as his name became better known and his income increased he gradually relocated to more commodious dwellings (albeit mostly rented). Honda named some seven locations that Shundei had lived in over a period of around two years, including Kikui-chō in Ushigome, Negishi, Yanaka-Hatsune, and Nippori Kanasugi.

It was after he had moved into Negishi, that Shundei finally became very popular and the magazine hacks started to arrive in droves. However, from about that time he showed an aversion to people and the front door was always locked, while his wife used the back door to come and go.

Often he would refuse to meet visitors, feigning that he was out, only to send a polite note explaining 'I do not like company;

please send a letter stating your business.' Only a few journalists were able to meet and speak to Shundei – most gave up in frustration. While they were used to the strange habits of novelists, Shundei's misanthropy was too much.

As it happens, though, his wife was a woman of considerable sagacity and Honda often went through her when negotiating manuscripts or pressing for something.

That said, it could be quite difficult even to meet the wife because the front door would be closed with strict-sounding notices hanging from it carrying such messages as 'No interviews granted due to illness,' 'Away on a trip,' and 'Journalists: all manuscript commission requests to be sent by letter; no interviews.' On more than one occasion even Honda was discouraged and left in disappointment.

As Shundei did not notify anyone of his new address when he moved, the journalists all had to search for him based on his mail.

'There might be a lot of journalists, but I'm probably the only one to talk with Shundei and joke with his wife,' boasted Honda.

My curiosity was growing steadily and I asked: 'Going by the photographs, Shundei seems quite a handsome chap. Is that how he actually looks?'

'Ha! Those photographs must be fakes. Shundei said they were taken when he was young, but it seems odd to me. He's just not that good looking. You could put it down to extreme puffiness and obesity brought on by lack of exercise. He's always lying down, you know. Although he's overweight, the skin on his face hangs down terribly, giving him the expressionless look of a Chinaman, while his eyes are clouded and turbid. I'd say he looks something like a drowned corpse. What's more, he's terrible at speaking and keeps his mouth shut. It makes you wonder how he could write such marvellous fiction.

'You remember that Uno Kōji novel *Hitodenkan*, right? Well Shundei is exactly like that. He lies down so much he could get bed sores and I'd say it's probably true he eats while in bed.

'Still, there's something peculiar. Even though he is so averse to company and is always in bed, there are rumours that he sometimes disguises himself and wanders around in the Asakusa area. And it's always at night. You'd think he was a robber or a bat. I wonder if he isn't really painfully shy. Perhaps he just doesn't want people to see his bloated body and face. The more famous he becomes, the more ashamed he is of his unsightly body. It could be he wanders secretly around in the thronging quayside at night instead of making friends and meeting visitors. That's the feeling I get based on his character and reading between the lines of what his wife says.'

Honda had created an image of Shundei with considerable eloquence. Finally he told me something very strange.

'You may be interested to know, Mr Samukawa, that I met the elusive Ōe Shundei the other day. He appeared so different that I didn't greet him, but I am sure it was Shundei.'

'Where? Where was this?' I asked instantly.

'In Asakusa Park. Actually, I was making my way home after having been out late and I may still have been a little drunk.'

Honda grinned and scratched his face.

'You know that Chinese restaurant Rai-Rai Ken? Well it was on that corner early in the morning when there are not many people about. I saw a fat person standing there in a clown's costume with a deep-red pointy hat handing out advertising leaflets. It sounds like something out of a dream, but it was Ōe Shundei. I stopped in surprise and was wondering if I should say something when he seemed to notice me too. But the face remained an expressionless blank and he then swivelled away and made off at great speed down the street opposite. I thought about going after him, but then realized that it might actually be out of order to greet him in that get up so I decided against it and just went home.'

Listening to Ōe Shundei's odd way of life, I had felt an unpleasant sensation as if I was having a nightmare. Then when I heard about him standing in Asakusa Park wearing a pointed hat and a clown's costume, for some reason I felt shocked and the hair on the back of my neck stood up.

I could not understand what the connection was between his appearance as a clown and the threatening letters to Shizuko (it seemed that Honda had met Shundei in Asakusa just at the time when the first of these letters arrived), but I knew that I could not just let it slide.

To confirm that the script in the threatening notes I was keeping for Shizuko was indeed Shundei's handwriting, I selected one page only from a section where the meaning was not clear and showed it to Honda.

Honda confirmed that the handwriting was Shundei's and he also said that the flourishes and style could only have been penned by Shundei. Honda knew the features of Shundei's handwriting because he had once tried to write a novel in his style, but he said that he found it impossible to copy that relentless, cloying approach. I knew what he meant. Having read a number of his letters in their entirety, I was even more aware than Honda of the distinctive trace of Shundei contained therein.

Using some flimsy pretext, I asked Honda if he could track down Shundei.

'Sure, leave it to me,' he accepted without fuss. Still, as that was not enough to set my mind at rest I decided to check the area around block 32 of Sakuragi-chō, in Ueno, which Honda had told me was where Shundei had lived.

# 4

The next day, I left a manuscript I had started to write where it lay and set out for Sakuragi-chō, where I stopped maids from the neighbourhood and trades people visiting local homes to ask them about the Ōe household. I was able to confirm the veracity of Honda's account, but I could not find out one jot more about Shundei's subsequent whereabouts.

As many of the homes in the area were middle-class establishments with their own gateways, the neighbours did not chat together as they would when living in more tightly packed cheaper dwellings and accordingly the most anybody could say was that the household had relocated without giving a destination. Of course, there was no doorplate bearing the name Ōe Shundei, so nobody knew that the house had been occupied by a famous author. As nobody even knew the name of the movers who had carted the luggage away in a truck, I had to return empty-handed.

With no other alternative available, every day I snatched quick breaks while working urgently on a manuscript and phoned Honda to inquire about the search, but it seemed there were no clues and the days passed by. While we were thus occupied, Shundei steadily pushed forward with his obsessive plot.

One day Oyamada Shizuko telephoned me at my lodgings and after telling me that something very worrying had occurred she asked me to come over. Apparently her husband was away and all of the house staff on whom she could rely were out on errands. It seems she had decided to use a public telephone rather than call from the house, and such was her extreme hesitation that she only had time to make the request before the three minutes elapsed and the line was lost.

I felt a little strange that she had thought to ask me over in this somewhat coquettish fashion with her husband fortuitously away and the servants out about their tasks.

I agreed to her request and went to her house, which was in Yama no Shuku, in Asakusa.

Tucked well down between two merchant buildings, the Oyamada home was an old building that resembled a dormitory from the past. While the Sumida River was not visible from the front, I thought that it probably flowed at the back. The building, which appeared to have been recently extended, differed from a dormitory in that it was surrounded by a very large and tasteless concrete wall (topped with glass shards to ward off thieves), while behind the main building arose a double storey block built in a Western style. The disharmony between the old, very Japanese looking building and these two structures gave an impression of moneyed but unrefined taste.

After presenting my card, I was shown to the parlour of the Western-style building by a young woman who seemed to be from the country. Shizuko was waiting there with a serious expression on her face.

She apologized many times over for her lack of propriety in having called me, and then assuming a low voice for some reason she said, 'First, please take a look at this' as she produced a document in an envelope. Looking behind as if afraid, she edged closer to me. It was of course a letter from Ōe Shundei, but as the content was slightly different from the documents she had received thus far I include it below:

*Shizuko, I can see the anguish you are in.*

*I am also aware that unbeknownst to your husband you are going to great lengths to track me down. However, it is no good so you may as well stop. Even if you had the courage to reveal my threatening letters to him and as a result the matter ended up in the hands of the police, you'll never discover my whereabouts. You only need to look at my novels to understand what a well-prepared fellow I am.*

*Now then, it is about time my prelude came to an end. The moment has arrived for this business of revenge to move to the second stage. First though, I should let you in a little on the background. You can probably broadly surmise how I was able to learn with such accuracy what you were doing each night. Since I found out where you were, I have been following you as closely as a shadow. You cannot see me at all, but I can observe you at every moment, whether you are at home or out about your business. I have become your very shadow. Even now as you read this letter trembling with fear, perhaps this shadow is staring at you from some corner of the room through narrowed eyes.*

*Naturally, as I observed your activities every night I had to see the intimacy between you and your husband and of course I felt extremely jealous.*

*Although this was something I did not allow for when I first brewed up my revenge scheme, it did not hinder my plan in the least. What is more, the jealousy even served as fuel to kindle the flames of my vengeful heart. Then I realized that if I made a slight adjustment to my plan it would better serve my objectives.*

*My original plan called for me to expose you to great torment and fear before eventually taking your life, but since recently having had to witness the intimacy between you and your husband I have come to think that before killing you it would probably be quite effective if I took the life of your beloved right before your eyes and then make it your turn after you have been given sufficient time to savour the tragedy. And that is what I have decided to do.*

*But you do not need to panic. I never rush things because it would be such a waste to move to the next step before you had fully relished the anguish produced by perusing my first letter.*

*Your vengeful devil (this late night of 16 March)*

On reading this horribly cruel letter I could not suppress a shudder. I sensed my hatred toward Ōe Shundei multiply.

But were I to give in to fear, who would comfort poor beleaguered Shizuko? There was nothing for it but to feign complaisance and explain to her repeatedly that the letter's threats were simply a novelist's fantasies.

'I entreat you to speak more softly.'

Shizuko was not heeding my earnest explanations. Her attention was focused elsewhere and from time to time she would stare fixedly at one spot in a way that suggested she was listening intently. Then she lowered her voice much as if someone were eavesdropping on us. Her lips lost so much colour that there was no contrast between them and her pale face.

'I think I could be going a little crazy. But was that real, do you think?'

Mouthing meaningless words in a whisper, it seemed Shizuko could perhaps have lost her mind.

'Did something happen?'

I too had been drawn in and was now talking in a very low voice.

'Hirata Ichirō is in this house.'

'Where?'

I looked at her blankly, unable to grasp her meaning.

Standing up suddenly, Shizuko blanched and beckoned me. I walked after her, becoming nervous myself. Noting my wristwatch, she had me remove it for some reason and then went back to place it on the table. Muffling our footsteps, we next moved down a short corridor to Shizuko's living room, which was in the Japanese-style building. As she opened the screen door, Shizuko seemed afraid that there might be some ruffian lurking immediately behind.

'It's a little odd, you know, to think that man would sneak into your house in broad daylight. Are you sure you aren't mistaken?'

After I had spoken, she made to stifle an impulsive gasp with her hand and then taking my hand she went to a corner of the room where she looked up at the ceiling and signalled to me to be quiet and listen.

We stood there for ten minutes our eyes locked together as we listened intently.

Although it was the middle of the day, there was not a sound in the room, which was deep within the large house, and such was the silence you could hear the blood beating in your ears.

After a while, Shizuko asked in a voice so low I could hardly hear her, 'Do you hear the timepiece ticking?'

'A timepiece? No, where is it?'

For a while she remained silent, listening attentively, then apparently reassured she said, 'I can't hear it now.'

Shizuko led me back to the room in the Western-style build-ing and with laboured breathing she then began to relate the following unusual events.

She had been doing a little needlework in the parlour, when the maid brought in the letter from Shundei quoted above. By this stage she could recognize his letters from just a glimpse of the envelope and she had an unpleasant feeling when she took the document, but she had to open it. With a heightened sense of uneasiness she fearfully cut the envelope and began to read.

When she realized that her husband was now involved, she

could not stay still. For no particular reason, she stood up and walked to the corner of the room. Just as she stopped in front of the wardrobe, she heard a very faint sound above her head that seemed almost like the noise made by a grub.

'I thought it might just be a ringing in my ears, but I stood completely still and listened and heard something that was not my ears ringing. It was a definite ticking like the sound that might be produced by metal touching against metal.'

Somebody must be concealed above the ceiling boards and this was the sound of that person's pocket watch marking out the seconds.

Probably she had been able to detect that ever-so-faint whisper of metal behind the ceiling because she just happened to be standing up, and so her ears were positioned closer to the ceiling, because the room was so quiet, and because nervousness had sharpened her senses. Thinking that perhaps the sound came from a timepiece in a different direction and that, much as with a light beam, reflection made it seem to emanate from behind the ceiling, she searched every nook and cranny but there was no clock or watch anywhere in the area.

Then she recalled a sentence from the letter: 'Even now as you read this letter trembling with fear, perhaps this shadow is staring at you from some corner of the room through narrowed eyes.' Her attention was drawn to a crack just there in the ceiling where the board had pulled back slightly. It seemed to her that she could see Shundei's eyes glinting narrowly in the pitch dark deep inside the crack.

'Hirata Ichirō, it's you in there isn't it?'

Shizuko suddenly felt a strange excitement. As if thrusting herself in front of her enemy, she was speaking to the person in the attic, all the time crying large tears.

'I don't care what happens to me. I'll do whatever you require. Kill me if you must. But please leave my husband alone.

I lied to him. It would be too terrible if on top of that he should die for my sake.'

Her voice was weak but she entreated with all her heart.

But there was no reply from above. The excitement faded and she stood there for a long time as if drained. But apart from the tick-tocking there in the attic, not the slightest sound could be heard. Deep within the darkness, the beast in the shadows held its breath as silent as a mute.

In that eerie silence she suddenly felt terribly frightened. Shizuko dashed out of the parlour and, unwilling to stay in the house for some reason, she ran out the front. Remembering me, she rushed to a nearby telephone booth.

As I listened to Shizuko's account, I couldn't help remembering a weird story by Ōe Shundei entitled 'Games in the Attic.' If the ticking sound Shizuko had heard was not a delusion and Shundei was concealed in there, it could mean that he had decided to put into practice the concepts of the story and this would be very typical of Shundei's behaviour.

Because I had read 'Games in the Attic,' I could not laugh off Shizuko's seemingly bizarre story and I too was beset by a great fear. I even seemed to see a bloated Ōe Shundei leering there in the darkness wearing a red pointed hat and a clown's costume.

**5**

After talking it over, I decided that, just like the amateur sleuth in 'Games in the Attic,' I would climb into the attic above Shizuko's parlour and see if I could find any trace of someone having been there, and if there were some trace I would try to determine exactly how the person had entered and exited.

Shizuko tried her best to stop me, saying 'Such an unpleasant thing . . . you couldn't possibly,' but I would not heed her and, as shown in Shundei's story, I removed the ceiling board inside the cupboard and climbed up inside the hole like an electrician. Apart from the maid who had come out to answer the door, there was no one else in the house, and as the maid appeared to be working in the kitchen I was not concerned about being spied by anybody.

The attic was not as beautiful as the one in Shundei's fiction.

This was an old house, but the attic was not terribly dirty because at the end of the year the cleaners had come in and removed the ceiling boards and washed them thoroughly. Still, the dust had gathered over the past three months, as had the spider webs. First, it was so dark you could not see a thing, so I borrowed a torch that was in Shizuko's house and, carefully navigating along the beams, I approached the spot in question. Gaps had opened up between the ceiling boards, which had perhaps curved back so much due to the cleaning. The light that shone up from below acted as a landmark. I had only gone a metre, but had already discovered something startling.

Although I had climbed thus into the attic, the truth is I thought it could not be as Shizuko said – that she must surely have imagined it. However, the reverse side of the ceiling boards did indeed carry the traces of someone having been there recently.

Suddenly, I felt a cold sensation. An indescribable shudder ran through me when I thought that Ōe Shundei, that poisonous spider of a man whom I knew only through his novels, had crawled through the attic in just the same fashion as I was now doing. I steeled myself and followed the footprints or handprints that had been left in the dust on the beams. At the place from which the ticking sound had supposedly emanated, the dust had indeed been considerably disturbed and there were signs that somebody had been there for a long time.

Preoccupied now, I began to stalk what appeared to be the traces left by Shundei. It seems that he had walked through more or less every part of the attic – the strange footprints were all over. In particular, above Shizuko's parlour and the bedroom she and her husband used some floorboards had gaps between them and the dust was very disturbed.

Just like the character in 'Games in the Attic,' I peeked down into the room below and it seemed entirely possible that Shundei had gazed in ecstasy there. The strange scene in the 'netherworld' visible through the cracks between the boards was truly beyond imagination. In particular, when I looked at Shizuko, who happened to be right below me, I was surprised at how strange a person can appear depending on the angle of vision.

We always look at each other side on and even the most self conscious person does not consider how he or she looks from above. How vulnerable we are! And precisely because of that vulnerability, those who make no effort to adorn themselves are exposed in a somewhat unflattering light. The depression between Shizuko's fringe and glistening chignon (from directly above the *marumage* bob had already lost its symmetry) was thin, but some dust had gathered there and it looked very dirty compared to the other pretty parts. As I was looking from straight above, I could see down past the nape that followed on from her coiffure into the valley formed between the collar of her kimono and her back. I could even see the bumps along her spine and also the poisonous red weal that painfully wound along her moist white skin down into the darkness and out of sight. Regarded from aloft, Shizuko seemed to lose some of her ladylike refinement and instead a certain strange obscenity she possessed loomed larger for me.

To see if any evidence of Ōe Shundei's presence remained, I directed the torch's light onto the ceiling boards and searched around, but the handprints and foot marks were unclear and naturally fingerprints could not be made out. Shundei had probably worn gloves and gone in stockinged feet, as set down in 'Games in the Attic.'

However, a small, mouse-coloured round object had fallen in a hard to see spot at the foot of a strut rising from the ceiling to a beam right above Shizuko's parlour. The faded metal object was hollowed out like a bowl and looked like a button. On its surface, the letters 'R.K. BROS. CO.' stood out in relief.

When I picked it up, I immediately thought of the shirt button in 'Games in the Attic,' but this was a somewhat unusual button. It looked as though it could be some sort of decoration on a hat, but I couldn't be sure. When I showed it to Shizuko later, she could only shake her head.

Naturally, I carefully sought to ascertain how Shundei had managed to sneak into the attic.

Following the traces of disturbance in the dust, I noticed that they stopped above the storeroom beside the entrance hall. The storeroom's rough ceiling boards shifted easily when I tried to lift them. Using a broken chair that had been thrown inside as a platform, I climbed down and made to open the storeroom door from the inside. The door had no lock and opened easily. Immediately outside was a concrete wall just a little higher than a person.

Perhaps Ōe Shundei had waited until no one was about, climbed over the wall (as noted above, the wall was topped by glass shards, but this would be no obstacle to a scheming intruder) and sneaked into the attic through the storeroom's lockless door.

Once I had fully grasped it all, I felt a little disappointed. I wanted to scorn the perpetrator for committing the childish prank of a delinquent. The odd mysterious fear disappeared, leaving only a real feeling of displeasure. (I would only learn later how mistaken I was to scorn the perpetrator.)

Beside herself with fear and anxious that her husband's life should not come into danger, Shizuko suggested going to the police even if it meant revealing her secret. However, I had begun to look down on our opponent and I calmed Shizuko by assuring her the perpetrator would not do anything so silly as to drip poison down from the ceiling, as in 'Games in the Attic,' and that even though he had sneaked into the attic this did not mean he could murder someone. Trying to frighten people like this was just the sort of childish thing Shundei would get up to and it seemed likely that he would make it appear as though he were perpetrating some crime. I consoled her that a mere novelist like him lacked any further ability to put his plans into action. To set her mind at rest, I promised to ask a friend who was keen on such things to watch the area around the wall outside the storeroom every night.

Shizuko said that fortunately there was a guest bedroom on

the second floor of the European-style section of the building
and that she would use some pretext or other to justify using
that as their bedroom for the time being. This part of the building did not have any chinks in the ceiling for prying eyes.

These defensive measures were put into action the following
day, but Ōe Shundei, the evil beast in the shadows, simply
ignored the makeshift ploys. Two days later, on 19 March, the
first victim was butchered, exactly as he had forewarned.
Oyamada Rokurō drew his last breath.

6

The letter advising of the impending murder of Oyamada had included the phrase: 'But you do not need to panic. I never rush things.' Then why had he perpetrated the crime in such haste just two days later? Or perhaps that had been a tactic – a phrase inserted into the letter in order to create a false sense of security. But it suddenly occurred to me that there could be another reason.

It was something I feared when I heard Shizuko pleading in tears for Oyamada's life after she heard the ticking watch and became convinced Shundei had sneaked into the attic. It seemed certain that when Shundei became aware of Shizuko's devotion to her husband his jealously had intensified and at the same time he had felt threatened. He might have thought: 'Right, if you love your husband so much, I'll finish him off quick rather than keep you waiting a long time.' Leaving that aside, in the case of the odd death of Oyamada Rokurō the body was discovered in extremely strange circumstances.

I first heard all the details after receiving a message from Shizuko and hastening to the Oyamada residence on the evening of the same day. On the previous day, he had returned from the company slightly earlier than normal and there was nothing particularly unusual about his appearance. After finishing his evening drink, Oyamada said he was going across the river to play go at his friend Koume's place and as it was a balmy evening he set off wearing simply a light Ōshima kimono and *haori* rather than a coat. This was at about seven in the evening.

As he was in no hurry, he strolled as usual by way of Azuma-bashi bridge and walked along the Mukōjima riverbank. He stayed at his friend's house until around midnight and then left on foot. It was all clear up to this point, but from there nothing was known.

Although Shizuko was up all night waiting, he did not come home, and given that she had just received a terrifying threat from Ōe Shundei she was very worried. As she waited for the dawn, she tried to contact everyone she could think of using the telephone and the servants, but there was no indication that he had been to any of these places. Naturally, she rang me, but I happened to have been out from the previous evening and as I did not return until the next night I did not hear anything about these events as they occurred.

Finally, the moment for Oyamada to show up for work arrived. As there was no sign of him, the company did its best to find him, but his whereabouts remained unknown. By this time, it was nearly noon. Just then, the Kisagata police called to report that Oyamada Rokurō had died in strange circumstances. A little to the north of the Kaminarimon gate train stop on the west side of the Azumabashi bridge, a path descends from the main riverbank walkway to a landing place for the ferry plying the route between the Azumabashi and Senju bridges. Recalling the era of the penny steamers, the ferry service was one of the Sumida River's tourist attractions. I often boarded the motor launch with no particular purpose, making the return trip between Kototoi and Shirahige bridges because I loved the old-time rural atmosphere conjured up by the traders, who brought picture books and toys on board, and who described their wares in time to the beat of the screw in the hoarse voice of a narrator who takes on all the roles in a silent movie. The landing place was a floating quay on the Sumida River, and the passenger waiting benches and toilets were all located on this wallowing boat platform. Having used that toilet myself, I knew it was just a box-like enclosure with a rectangular opening in the wooden floor that opened directly on to the muddy river, which coiled along thickly about a foot below.

Just as on a steam train or a ship, there was nothing in the toilet to hold up waste matter and accordingly it was indeed clean, but if you stared intently down from the rectangular hole into the eddying fathomless black water, you could occasionally see bits of flotsam appear on one side of the hole and float out of sight on the other side like micro-organisms viewed in a microscope. It gave one a strange feeling.

About eight o'clock in the morning of 20 March, the proprietress of one of the merchant family stalls in Asakusa's Nakamise arcade came to the Azumabashi ferry landing place on her way to Senju on business and while she was waiting for the vessel to arrive she went into the toilet. Immediately after, there was a scream and the woman came flying out.

When the elderly ticket collector asked her what had happened, she told him that she had seen a man's face looking up at her from the blue water directly under the rectangular hole.

At first the ticket collector thought it might be a prank played by one of the crew (there had been some peeping Tom incidents in the water from time to time), but he went into the toilet anyway to investigate, whereupon he indeed saw a human face floating there about a foot directly under the hole. Waving to and fro with the water's motion, half the face would disappear only to pop up again. 'So help me, he looked just like one of them wind-up dolls,' the ticket collector said later.

When he realized it was a corpse, the old man immediately got into a fluster and shouted out to the young fellows among the customers waiting for the ferry at the landing place.

Enlisting the aid of a strapping chap from the fish shop and some other young men, he attempted to lift up the dead body, but they were unable to pull him up through the hole in the toilet. Accordingly, they went outside and used a pole to prod the corpse out into the open water. Strangely, they discovered that the cadaver was stark naked, but for a pair of undershorts.

There was something unusual because this was a man around forty in rude health and it seemed unlikely that he would have been swimming in the Sumida River in this weather. Furthermore, a closer look revealed that his back had what looked to be a wound from a knife and the corpse contained relatively little water for a drowned man.

When it emerged this was a murder case rather than a death by drowning the commotion intensified. Then another queer thing happened when the corpse was lifted out of the water.

Under the instructions of an officer who had rushed from the Hanakawado police station after hearing the news, one of the young fellows at the landing place grasped the sodden hair of the cadaver and made to lift it up, but the hair slid smoothly away from the scalp. It was such an unpleasant feeling that the young man let go with a cry. It seemed odd that the hair should peel away so easily even though the body did not appear to have been in the water all that long, but a closer look revealed that what had appeared to be hair was in fact a wig and the man's head was completely bald.

This was the wretched death of Oyamada Rokurō, Shizuko's husband and director of Roku-Roku Trading Company.

After having been stripped naked, Rokurō's bald head had been covered with a fluffy wig and the corpse dumped into the river beneath Azumabashi. Furthermore, although the corpse had been discovered in the water, there was no sign that water had been ingested. The fatal injury was a wound inflicted by a sharp instrument to the back, in the section near the left lung.

Given that there were a number of other shallower stab wounds, it seemed certain that the criminal had stabbed the body multiple times.

According to the police surgeon's examination, the fatal wound had probably been inflicted around one o'clock that morning, but as the corpse was not clothed and there were no belongings, the police were unable to identify it. Luckily, someone who knew Oyamada by sight appeared around noon and the police immediately telephoned the Oyamada residence and the trading company.

When I visited that night, there was considerable confusion at the Oyamada home, which was thronged with relatives from the Oyamada side, employees of Roku-Roku Trading Company, and friends of the deceased. Shizuko said that she had just returned from the police station and she looked around aimlessly amidst a circle of those paying their respects.

Oyamada's corpse had not yet been handed over by the police. Under the circumstances, it had to undergo an autopsy, and accordingly the white cloth on the dais in front of the family Buddhist altar was occupied only by a hastily arranged mortuary tablet on which offerings of incense burned sadly.

From Shizuko and the trading company staff, I gained the full account of the discovery of the corpse as detailed above. When it occurred to me that I had caused this deplorable event, having scorned Shundei two or three days earlier and stopped Shizuko from notifying the police, I felt such shame and regret I wanted to leave.

It seemed to me that Ōe Shundei must be the criminal. When Oyamada was walking past Azumabashi after leaving Koume's house, Shundei must have pushed him down to the dark landing place, struck him with a weapon and thrown the body into the river. Surely there could be no doubt that Shundei was the perpetrator. In terms of timing, Honda had indicated that

Shundei was wandering around the Asakusa vicinity, and Shundei had even predicted Oyamada's murder.

Still, it was very strange that Oyamada had been quite naked and wearing an odd wig. If indeed this was the handiwork of Shundei, why had he done such an outlandish thing?

In order to discuss with Shizuko the secret we alone knew, I waited for the right moment then approached her and asked her into another room. Much as if she had been awaiting this, Shizuko bowed to the company and followed me in. Once out of sight of the guests, she cried out my name softly and suddenly clung to me. She looked fixedly at my chest. The long lashes glittered and the swelling in the space between her eyelids turned into large tears that coursed down her pale cheeks. The tears welled up one after another and flowed down ceaselessly.

Shizuko's tears were subsiding, but now I was overcome with emotion and taking her hand in mine I apologized over and over, pressing her hand as if to give her strength.

'I don't know what to say. It's all due to my carelessness. It didn't occur to me that he had the ability to carry this out. It's all my fault. I'm so sorry . . .'

That was the first time I felt Shizuko's body. I shall never forget that even in that situation it seemed that her core was aflame despite her pale tenderness and I was acutely aware of the wondrous touch of her warm, nimble fingers.

When Shizuko had stopped crying, I asked: 'So did you report that threatening letter to the police?'

'No, I wasn't sure what I should do.'

'So you still haven't said anything then?'

'No, I haven't. I wanted to discuss things with you.'

It seemed strange when I thought about it later, but at that time I was still holding her hand. Shizuko left her hand in mine and remained leaning against me.

'You still think it was his doing, don't you?'

43

'Yes, I do. And last night something strange happened.'

'Something strange?'

'Well, I shifted our bedroom to the second floor of the European part of the building, as you suggested. It put me at my ease to think that we would no longer be spied upon, but it seems as if he was peeping after all . . .'

'Where from, may I ask?'

'From outside – through the window.'

Her eyes opening wide as she remembered the fear of the moment, Shizuko haltingly recounted what had happened.

'I went to bed around twelve o'clock last night, but I was very worried because my husband hadn't come home. All alone in that high-ceilinged Western-style room I became afraid and it seemed to me I was being watched from every corner. One of the window blinds had not been fully lowered, and the foot or so left open revealed the pitch blackness outside. Even though I was afraid, for some reason my eyes seemed terribly drawn in that direction, when all of a sudden a person's face loomed vaguely into view.'

'Are you sure it wasn't a figment of your imagination?'

'It soon disappeared, but even now I am sure that I was not seeing things. The dishevelled hair was pressed up against the glass and I can still see those eyes staring up at me from the down turned face.'

'Was it Hirata?'

'I don't know . . . but there couldn't possibly be anyone else who would do such a thing.'

After this exchange, we decided that Oyamada's killer must be Hirata Ichirō (Ōe Shundei) and we agreed to go to the police together and tell them that he was plotting to murder Shizuko next and ask for their protection.

The detective in charge of this case was a law graduate named Itosaki, and fortunately he was a member of Crime

Hounds, a group composed of murder-mystery writers, doctors, and legal professionals. Accordingly, when Shizuko and I went to the investigation headquarters at Kisagata, rather than treating us stiffly – as a detective ordinarily would with the family of the victim – he listened to us kindly as a friend.

It seems that he was very alarmed by the case and that he also felt a considerable interest in it. He said that he would do his best to find Ōe Shundei and promised to protect Shizuko fully by assigning a detective to guard the Oyamada home and increasing the number of patrols. When I told the detective that the photos of Ōe Shundei now in circulation were not good likenesses, he contacted Honda to obtain an expert description of the suspect.

7

For about the following month, the constabulary exerted their all in the search for Ōe Shundei and I too did my utmost to establish his whereabouts, asking everyone I met, including Honda and other newspaper journalists and magazine writers, if they had any clue. But it was as if Shundei had woven some kind of spell – there was no trace of him.

It was not as if he were alone; there was his wife to slow him down, so where could the two of them be hiding? Could he, as Inspector Itosaki conjectured, have concocted a plan to smuggle them both on board a vessel and slip off to a distant land?

But the strange thing was that after the bizarre death of Rokurō, the threatening letters suddenly ceased. Perhaps frightened by the police search, Shundei had put off the next step in his scheme – the murder of Shizuko – and was intent only on staying out of sight. Yet, surely a man like him would have expected something like this. If so, then he might be lying low somewhere in Tokyo quietly waiting for a chance to kill Shizuko.

The head of the Kisagata police station ordered his men to search the area near 32 Sakuragi-chō in Ueno, which was Shundei's last known residence. Although I had attempted the same, the experts were able after great effort to discover the transport company that had moved Shundei's belongings (this was a small firm from around Kuromon, far from Ueno), and they then tracked down his next address.

The outcome of the inquiry was that after decamping from Sakuragi-chō, Shundei had gradually relocated to seedier addresses, including Yanagishima-chō in Honjo-ku and Mukōjima Suzaki-chō. The final residence was a squalid rental house in Sugisaki-chō that looked just like a barracks and was squeezed between two factories. He had paid several months' rent in advance and when the detective went to investigate the landlord thought that Shundei was still living there. However, when they looked inside there were no belongings and the dust-covered interior was in such a state there was no telling when he had left. Nothing much could be gained from asking the neighbours because there were no observant housewives around – only the factories on either side.

As a specialist who in his heart enjoyed such things, Honda grew very enthusiastic as he became more aware of the situation. Since he had met Shundei once in Asakusa Park, in between his work gathering articles he began to sedulously emulate the activities of a private eye.

First, given that Shundei had been handing out fliers, Honda visited one or two advertising agencies in the Asakusa area to see if they had employed a man looking like Shundei, but to his chagrin in busy times these firms would hire vagrants from Asakusa Park on a temporary basis, fitting them up with costumes and paying them by the day, and so a description of Shundei did not prompt any recollection of him and the suggestion was that surely he had been one of the vagrants.

Honda next took to wandering around Asakusa Park late at night peering in at each of the benches hidden in the dark shadows under the trees or staying at cheap lodging houses that vagrants might use in the Honjo area, striking up friendly chats with the guests and asking whether they had laid eyes on a man who looked like Shundei. He certainly went to great pains but he was unable to obtain even the smallest clue.

Honda came to my lodgings about once a week to recount his tales of hardship. Then, one time he assumed the knowing countenance of the beaming god Daikoku and told me the following.

'Samukawa, just recently I learned about this freak show and I came up with a wonderful idea. I expect you know that lately popular attractions at these shows include "the spider woman" and "the woman with only a neck and no body." Well, there's a similar spectacle where conversely the person has only a body and no neck. There's a long box with three compartments, two sections of which generally contain the torso and legs of a sleeping woman. The section above the torso is empty; although you should be able to see the body from the neck up, it isn't visible at all. What you have then is the neckless corpse of a woman laid out, but every so often the legs and hands twitch to prove that it is alive. It's an eerie and erotic spectacle. The trick is that a mirror is placed at an angle so that the part at the back looks empty. Though it's a bit childish, of course.

'Well, once when I was at Edogawa-bashi in Ushigome, I saw one of these "headless human" freak shows in an empty lot at the corner as I crossed the bridge toward Gokokuji. However, this time the all-body human wasn't a woman, but a very fat man in a clown's costume covered with gleaming black grime.'

At this point, Honda assumed a somewhat tense expression and teasingly fell silent for a while, but after confirming that he had sufficiently piqued my curiosity he resumed his story.

'You know what I thought, don't you? It struck me that to be hired as the "headless man" in such a freak show would be a brilliant way for someone to completely cover their tracks while at the same time being exposed to the gaze of all and sundry. By hiding the tell-tale section from the neck up, he would be able to sleep all day. Isn't this just the sort of fantastical method Ōe

Shundei would dream up? What's more, Shundei has written a lot of freak show stories and he delights in this type of thing.'

'What happened?'

I encouraged Honda to go on, though his calmness made me think that he had not actually found Shundei.

'I immediately went to Edogawa-bashi to have a look, and fortunately the show was still there. After paying the entrance fee, I went inside and stood in front of that fat "headless man," and tried to think of a way to see his face. Then it occurred to me that the man would have to go to the toilet a few times every day. So I waited patiently for him to go to relieve himself. After a while, the few customers drifted out and I was left alone. But I stood there waiting steadfastly. Then the "headless man" clapped his hands together twice.

'That's odd, I thought. Just then one of the barkers came over to tell me there would be a small break and asked me to step outside. Realizing this was it, I went out, sneaked round behind the tent and peeped in through a rent in the fabric. Aided by the barker, the "headless man" was getting out of the box and of course he had a head. Running to a corner of the earth floor beyond the spectator seats, he began to relieve himself. So the clap I'd heard earlier was a signal that he needed to pee. Very funny, don't you think? Ha, ha, ha.'

'What is this, a comedy routine? Come on, be serious now.'

Seeing that I was a little angry, Honda's face became serious and he explained,

'Well I was mistaken. It was a completely different person . . . but it shows you the lengths I went to. It's just one example of the great pains I've taken in the search for Shundei.'

Just as in this humorous digression, no matter how long we searched for Shundei, we were unable to perceive any glimmer of hope.

However, I must note here one unusual fact that came to

light that I thought could be a key to solving the case. When I saw the wig worn by Oyamada's corpse, it occurred to me that perhaps it could have come from the Asakusa area. After investigating all the wigmakers in the vicinity, I found an establishment called Matsui in Sensoku-machi that seemed to match. However, although the shop's hairpieces were exactly like that on the dead man's body, I was surprised – no, completely dumbfounded – when the wigmaker told me that the person who had ordered the wig was not Ōe Shundei but Oyamada Rokurō himself.

The person's description closely resembled Oyamada, and the man gave his name as Oyamada when placing the order, and when the wig was ready (this was near the end of last year) he himself came to collect it. At the time, Oyamada explained that he wished to hide his bald pate, but then why was it that not even his wife had seen him wearing the wig while he was alive? No matter how much I thought about it, I couldn't unravel this odd mystery.

Meanwhile, after Rokurō's bizarre murder, the relationship between Shizuko (now a widow) and myself rapidly became more intimate. Under the circumstances, I stood as both an advisor and a guardian to her. Once the relatives on Oyamada's side had learned of my consideration in searching the attic, they could not turn a cold shoulder to me, while Inspector Itosaki said that it was truly fortunate if it came to that and encouraged me to visit the Oyamada home when I could to comfort the widow with my presence. Accordingly, it became possible for me to come and go in the house without reserve.

I have written above that from the first meeting Shizuko had shown me no little affection as an avid fan of my novels, but a more complex relationship had now developed between us and it seemed entirely natural that she should depend on me more than anyone.

We were meeting frequently now. When it was borne in

upon me that she had become a widow, the pale passion – the attraction of a body that looked so delicate it might disappear at any moment, and that yet had a strange strength – no longer seemed something distant, but suddenly pressed in upon me swathed in living colour. In particular, after I happened to find a small foreign-made riding whip in her bedroom, troubling appetites flamed up in me with a frightening force, as if oil had been poured on fire.

Thoughtless though it was, I pointed at the whip and asked: 'Was your husband a horseman?'

She seemed to gasp and blanched immediately. Then her face gradually reddened as if burning. She answered very quietly: 'No.'

It was then that I managed to solve the odd riddle of her livid scar. I recalled that each time I saw the wound its position and shape seemed to differ slightly. I had thought it strange at the time, but it didn't occur to me that her good-natured bald husband might be an awful sex fiend.

Not only that. Today – exactly a month after Rokurō's death – search as I might I could not see that ugly wormlike scar on the nape of Shizuko's neck. Combining this with what I recalled from the past, I was sure that this was not a figment of my imagination without needing to hear a clear confession from her.

But even knowing this, why was it that I was troubled by such unbearable lust? Terribly shameful though it would be, perhaps I was a sexual deviant just like Oyamada . . .

# 8

As 20 April was the day for commemorating Oyamada's death, Shizuko went to the temple and then spent the evening at a Buddhist ceremony for the departed accompanied by relatives and friends of the deceased. I was also present. Two new events occurred that evening (even though they were entirely different in nature, as is made clear later, there was a strange and fatalistic link between them) that moved me so much I shall probably remember it all my life.

I was walking beside Shizuko down the dark corridor. I had stayed after all the guests had gone home so that I could talk alone with Shizuko (about the search for Shundei). I thought it would not do to stay too long, what with the servants being there and everything, so I said goodnight at perhaps 11:00 p.m. and returned to my home in a taxi that Shizuko had summoned. She walked alongside me down the corridor toward the hallway to say goodbye. There were a number of glass windows in the corridor that faced on to the garden and as we passed one of them Shizuko suddenly screamed in fear and clung to me.

Surprised, I asked, 'What is it? Did you see something my dear?'

Still grasping me firmly with one hand, she pointed at the window with the other.

I gasped at first, thinking of Shundei, but I soon realized it was nothing. Looking through the glass into the garden, I saw a white dog among the trees. It scratched at the fallen leaves and disappeared into the darkness.

'It's a dog, just a dog. There's nothing to be afraid of.'

I am not sure what it was that possessed me, but I was patting Shizuko on the shoulders as I said this, trying to calm her down. Even when she realized there was nothing out of the ordinary, one of Shizuko's arms was embracing my back and when I sensed her warmth spreading inside my body I drew her close and stole a kiss from those Mona Lisa lips, which were lifted slightly by her eye teeth.

Whether it was fortunate or unfortunate for me I do not know, but she did not seek to evade me. Indeed, I even detected a diffident pressure in the hand that embraced me.

The feeling we had of doing something wrong was all the more keen given that this was the day of commemoration for the deceased. We spoke not a word from then until I got into the taxi, and I recall that we even avoided each other's eyes.

We parted and the taxi moved off, but all I could think of was Shizuko. The touch of her mouth lingered on my hot lips and I could still sense the warmth of her body against my pounding chest.

While joy began to soar within me, I also felt a deep sense of remorse. My heart was a tangle of the two, like some complex fabric. I was oblivious of just where the taxi now was, how it was moving, and of the view that lay beyond.

Strangely though, even in that situation I had become intensely aware of a certain small object. Swayed by the vehicle's motion and thinking only of Shizuko, I was staring straight ahead. I could not help but notice a tiny object moving slightly exactly in the centre of my line of sight. At first, I looked without paying attention, but gradually my interest grew.

'Why,' I wondered vaguely, 'why am I staring so much?'

Then, I became aware of what it was.

The all too coincidental matching of two objects was what puzzled me.

Hunched forward in front of me was the driver, a large man wearing an old navy jacket suitable for spring weather. Beyond the fleshy shoulders, the two hands gripping the steering wheel moved jerkily and they were covered by a pair of refined gloves that seemed at odds with the coarse fingers within.

My eye had also been drawn because these were winter gloves and thus out of season, but more than this it was the ornamental button closure on the gloves . . . finally, the moment of enlightenment came. The round metallic object I had found in the attic of the Oyamada household was the ornamental button from a glove.

I had mentioned the metallic object to Inspector Itosaki, but as I did not happen to have it on me then, and all the signs pointed clearly to Ōe Shundei being the criminal, neither of us had considered this as a material piece of evidence. It should still be in the pocket of my winter waistcoat.

It had not occurred to me that the object could be the ornamental button of a glove. However, thinking about it now, it seemed all too likely that the criminal had worn gloves in order not to leave any fingerprints and that the button had fallen off without the criminal realizing.

The showy button on the driver's glove had thus taught me the provenance of the object I had picked up in the attic, but it held a far more alarming significance. Why was it that the button was so similar in shape and size? Not only that, why had the button on the driver's right hand glove been torn off leaving only the metallic seat of the hook closure? If the metallic object I had picked up in the attic matched this hook closure fitting, what would it mean?

'I say, you there . . .' I called out to the driver suddenly. 'Would you mind letting me see those gloves please?'

The driver seemed somewhat taken aback by my strange request, but he slowed the taxi, took off both gloves without ado, and passed them to me.

The surface of the button on the complete glove bore the inscription 'R.K. BROS. CO.', the letters I had previously seen, and the dimensions were the same. My alarm grew greater and I began to feel a strange fear.

Having passed me the gloves, the driver focused on the road without looking in any other direction. As I stared at his very stout form from behind, a wild thought came into my head.

'Ōe Shundei . . .'

I said it as if to myself, but loud enough for the driver to hear. Then I looked intently at the reflection of his face in a small mirror mounted above the driver's seat. But of course it was only my fantasy. The driver's expression showed not the slightest change. What is more, Ōe Shundei was not the type to carry out such a Lupin-like trick. However, when the taxi arrived at my lodging, I had him keep the change and began to ask some questions.

'Do you remember when this button came off?'

The driver replied with an odd look on his face, 'It was torn off from the start. I got it from someone, see. The button had come off, but it was still new, so Mr Oyamada, him that's dead now, he gave it to me.'

'Mr Oyamada did?' I blurted out, considerably surprised. 'The man from the house I've just left, you mean?'

'Yes, that's right. He treated me well when he was alive – it was mostly me that took him to the company and picked him up.'

'When did you start wearing these?'

'Well, they were given to me in winter, but as they were such good quality it seemed a pity to use them and I decided to look after them. Then my old gloves got damaged and today I pulled them down to use for driving for the first time. If I don't wear gloves, the steering wheel slips. But why are you asking?'

'Oh, I've got my own reasons. I wonder if you would sell them to me my good man?'

In the end, I purchased the gloves from him for a hefty consideration. After entering my room, I took out the metallic object I had found in the attic and it was exactly the same size and fitted into the metallic seat of the hook enclosure perfectly.

As noted above, this matching of the two objects seemed all too coincidental.

That Ōe Shundei and Oyamada Rokurō had worn gloves with the same ornamental markings on the hook closure and that the metal button that had fallen off matched exactly the closure's metal seat seemed unthinkable.

I later took the glove to be examined at Izumiya, a premier importer of Western goods located in Tokyo's Ginza. This type of glove was apparently rare within our shores: it might well have been manufactured in England, and R.K. Bros. Co. did not have a single outlet in Japan. Given what the owner of Izumiya had told me and that Oyamada had been overseas until September of last year, it seemed Rokurō was the owner of the glove and that therefore the ornamental button that had fallen off had been dropped by him. It seemed impossible that Ōe Shundei could have obtained such gloves in Japan or that he would just happen to have owned the same gloves as Oyamada.

'So what does that mean?'

Leaning on the desk with my head in my hands I mumbled oddly to myself over and over 'it means that . . . it means that . . .', while at the same time massaging my temples in a desperate attempt to focus my concentration to the core of my being and achieve some solution.

Finally, a strange idea came into my head. Yama no Shuku was a long, narrow district and as the Oyamada household was located in the part adjoining the Sumida River it naturally had to touch the river as it flowed past. When I went to the Oyamada household I had from time to time looked at the Sumida River from the window of the Western-style wing without thinking much about it, but now, I was struck by a new significance as if I had discovered the waterway for the first time.

A large letter 'ʊ' appeared in the swirling mist in my head.

The upper left section of the letter contained Yama no Shuku, while Ko-ume machi (where Rokurō's go partner lived) was in the upper right section.

The lower section of the 'ʊ' corresponded exactly to Azumabashi. Even now, we were convinced that Rokurō had left the upper right section that evening and travelled to the left part of the ʊ's trough, where he had been killed by Shundei. But we had not taken into account the river's current. The Sumida River flowed from the upper section of the 'ʊ' to its lower section. It seemed more natural to suppose that rather than the corpse being at the site of the murder, it had floated downstream after being thrown in, reached the ferry landing site under Azumabashi and come to a halt in the eddying current.

The body had floated down. It had floated down . . . But where had it floated from? Where had the fatal weapon been used? I found myself sinking further and further into the delusional mire.

# 9

I kept thinking about it night after night. Even Shizuko's allure seemed less powerful than this monstrous suspicion and as I became more and more obsessed by these bizarre fantasies it was as if I had somehow forgotten about Shizuko.

During that time I questioned Shizuko twice in order to confirm something, but she must have thought it strange because after completing this business I told her I had to leave urgently and rushed home. Indeed, her face seemed quite sad and forlorn when she saw me off in the entrance hall.

In just five days, I created an incredible delusion. As I still have the statement I wrote to send to Inspector Itosaki, I shall spare myself the trouble of detailing this delusion by reproducing the statement below and inserting some additional comments. The deductions therein are of a sort that it would probably have been impossible to assemble without the imaginative ability of a crime writer. I later came to realize that it contained something of profound significance.

*. . . When I realised that the metallic object I picked up in the attic above Shizuko's parlour in the Oyamada household had to have fallen from the closure of Oyamada Rokurō's glove, I recalled a series of disparate facts that had caused me disquiet. These included the fact that Oyamada's corpse wore a wig; that this hair-piece he had adorned himself with had been ordered by Oyamada himself (for reasons I note*

*below, it did not trouble me that the body had been unclothed); that Hirata's threatening letters had stopped at the same time as the bizarre death of Oyamada Rokurō, much as if by arrangement; and that belying appearances Oyamada had been a terrible sadist (though appearances are often deceiving in such cases). It may seem that these facts were a coincidental collection of oddities, but when I thought about it intensely I realized that they each pointed to the one thing.*

*When I became aware what that was, I started to gather together the materials to further confirm my deductions. First, I visited the Oyamada home and after obtaining the permission of Oyamada's wife I searched his study, for nothing tells you so much about a person's traits and secrets than his or her study. Unconcerned about what Mrs Oyamada might be thinking, I spent about half a day looking through book cabinets and drawers. I discovered that one section alone of the book cabinets was locked very securely. I asked for the key and was told that when he was alive Oyamada always carried it about with him on his watch chain and that on the day of his death he left the house with it in his waistband. As there was no other way, I eventually obtained Mrs Oyamada's consent to break open the door to the book cabinet.*

*Inside I found it was full of Oyamada's diaries for the past several years, documents contained in a number of bags, bundles of letters, and books. After searching through them one by one, I discovered three documents connected with this case. The first was the diary for the year in which he had married Shizuko. The following phrases were inscribed in red ink in the margin of the entry three days prior to the wedding ceremony: '. . . Know about relationship with youth called Hirata Ichirō. But along the way Shizuko came to dislike the boy and no matter what methods he employed she was unresponsive. Next, she used opportunity of father's bankruptcy to hide from Hirata. All well and good. Don't intend to rake up the past.'*

*Thus, by some means Rokurō had known all about his wife's secret from the start of their marriage. In addition, he had not said a single word of this to his wife.*

*The second document was 'Games in the Attic,' the collection of short stories written by Ōe Shundei. I was very surprised to find such a volume in the study of an entrepreneur such as Oyamada Rokurō. In fact, I could not believe my eyes until his wife Shizuko told me that he had been quite a fan of fiction. The frontispiece of the short story collection included a collotype portrait of Shundei and I was very interested to see that the author was credited in the colophon under his real name, Hirata Ichirō.*

*The third document was issue twelve of volume six of* Shin Seinen, *published by Hakubunkan. This magazine for younger readers did not contain a story by Shundei, but it did reproduce a photograph of his manuscript in the frontispiece without any reduction in size. This image commanded half a page and the caption in the margin read 'Ōe Shundei's handwriting.' The strange thing is that when a light was shone on this reproduction, the thick art paper everywhere reflected marks something like those that would be left by a fingernail. It seemed clear that someone had laid a thin sheet of paper on this photograph and traced Shundei's handwriting over and over with a pencil. It frightened me to see that my speculations continued to hit true.*

*The same day I requested Mrs Oyamada to search for the gloves that Rokurō had brought back from overseas. The search took considerable time, but eventually a glove was found that matched exactly the dimensions of the glove that I had purchased from the taxi driver. When she handed the glove to me, Mrs Oyamada said with a troubled look that she was sure there had been another glove exactly the same. If you so desire, I can at any moment produce these pieces of evidence, including the diary, the collection of short stories, the magazine, the glove, and the metallic object I picked up in the attic.*

*There are a number of other facts that I have ascertained, but based only on the key points noted above I think it seems clear that Oyamada Rokurō had a most peculiar character, and that behind his friendly mask he was energetically carrying out a ghoulish plot. Perhaps we were too conscious of the name Ōe Shundei. Being aware of Shundei's blood-thirsty works and his bizarre lifestyle, we may have arbitrarily decided that only he could have committed such a crime. How could he have so completely concealed himself? Does it not seem somewhat strange that he should be the criminal? If he is innocent, it could be that he is so difficult to track down simply because his misanthropy (an aversion that becomes more severe the more his fame grows) led him to cover his trail. It may well be as you once said that he has fled overseas. He could be puffing away on a water pipe in some corner of Shanghai passing himself off as a Chinese. Even if this is not the case and Shundei is the criminal, how could we explain him forgetting the main purpose of a detailed revenge plot put together over months and years with such tenacity and suddenly giving up after killing Oyamada, who was simply a diversion along the way? Anyone who knew his fiction and lifestyle would think this very unnatural and unlikely. Moreover, there is something much clearer. How is it that he could have dropped the button from Oyamada's glove in that attic? Given that this foreign-made glove was unobtainable in Japan and that the ornamental button had been pulled off the glove presented to the taxi driver, it would surely be illogical to think that it was Ōe Shundei rather than Oyamada who had been lurking in the attic (if I say it was Oyamada, you may ask whether he would give such a vital piece of evidence to a taxi driver even unwittingly; but as I note later that is because he was not committing any particular crime from a legal perspective; it was simply a sort of game for someone who enjoyed weird things; thus, even if the glove button was torn off and left behind in the attic, that would be of no consequence to him because he had no need to worry whether the button had fallen off while he was walking in the attic or whether it would serve as evidence).*

*There is still other information that ought to rule out Shundei from the crime. That the evidence mentioned above, including the diary, Shundei's short story collection, and Shin Seinen, was in the lockable book cabinet in Oyamada's study and that Oyamada always kept the only key to this lock on his person proves that he was involved* in an underhanded piece of mischief. Even if we pause and consider that Shundei could have attempted to cast suspicion on Oyamada by forging these items and placing them in his book cabinet, it seems completely impossible. First, the diary was not something that could be forged and only Oyamada was able to lock and unlock the book cabinet. Although we have thus far believed Ōe Shundei–Hirata Ichirō was the criminal, if we take everything into consideration we must conclude that surprisingly enough he was not a presence in this case from the very start. We could only have come to believe that he was the criminal due to the truly amazing deception of Oyamada Rokurō. It surprises us completely to learn that while this wealthy man had a childishness manifested in the detailed scheme noted above, beneath that mask of benevolence he transformed into a terrible fiend once in the bedroom and lashed the fair Shizuko repeatedly with his foreign-made riding whip. However, there are many instances in which the benevolence of a virtuous man and the guile of a fiend have resided together in one person. Indeed, the more benevolent and appealing to others a person is, the easier it is for the devil within to find disciples.

Now then, let me tell you what I think. About four years ago, Oyamada Rokurō travelled to Europe on business, where he lived for about two years. He was chiefly in London, but he also stayed in another two or three cities. I think it may have been in one of these metropolises that his evil habits budded and were fostered (I have heard rumours of his situation in London from an employee of Roku-Roku Trading). It seems to me that when he returned from abroad in September of the year before last his stubborn depravity turned on to his beloved bride Shizuko and the savage fury began, for I detected the unpleasant scar on the nape of her neck at our first meeting in October last year.

Once one has become accustomed to this type of depravity, the illness progresses with frightening rapidity, just as with morphine addiction.

*A new, more intense stimulation becomes necessary. What yielded satisfaction yesterday does not serve today and you come to think that today's measures will not be sufficient tomorrow. I think you will agree that it is easy to conceive that in a similar fashion Oyamada found he was no longer able to achieve satisfaction just from whipping his wife Shizuko. In a frenzy, he had to pursue a new stimulus. Right about that time he somehow became aware of a work of fiction called 'Games in the Attic' written by Ōe Shundei, and perhaps after the first reading he decided that he would like to enact the bizarre content. At any rate, he seems to have discovered a strange sense of affinity. He had found someone else who suffered from the same odd malady. The well-worn spine of the book suggests the fervour with which he read Shundei's short story collection. In this fiction, Shundei repeatedly describes the peculiar pleasure of peeping through a crack at someone alone (in particular, a woman) while remaining completely undetected. How easy it is to imagine the sympathy Oyamada must have felt when he discovered this, for him, new pastime. Quickly he copied the hero of Shundei's fiction, becoming himself the one playing in the attic. He dreamed up the scheme of sneaking into the space above the ceiling of his own home to peep at his wife when she was alone.*

*As there is a considerable distance from the gate of the Oyamada house to the entrance hall, it would require no artifice whatsoever when coming home to slip around the side of the entrance hall and into the storeroom unbeknownst to the servants and from there to pass along over the ceiling to the space above Shizuko's parlour. I suspect that Rokurō's frequent evening trips to play go with Koume may have been a way of accounting for the time when he was actually amusing himself in the attic.*

*Meanwhile, this devoted reader of 'Games in the Attic' probably discovered that the real name of the author was Hirata Ichirō, and began to suspect that this was almost certainly the same person who had been jilted by Shizuko and who bore a deep-seated grudge against* her for it. He would then have screened all sorts of articles and gossip related to Ōe Shundei to learn that Shundei was the same person who had formerly been Shizuko's lover, that he had a very misanthropic lifestyle, and that by this stage he had already stopped writing and even disappeared leaving no trace. Thus at one and the same time Oyamada had discovered through the one volume of 'Games in the Attic' someone who shared his malady and who was also an arch-rival of his love who ought to be hated. Based on all this knowledge, he came up with a truly alarming piece of mischief.

Of course, prying through a chink at Shizuko by herself would certainly have piqued his inordinate curiosity, but it is unlikely that his sadomasochistic character would have been satisfied by such a mild pastime alone. The preternaturally sharp creative abilities of this sick man would have sought for a new, crueller approach to substitute for the crack of the whip. Finally, he hit upon the unprecedented drama of Hirata Ichirō's threatening letters. He had already obtained the photo print at the start of issue twelve of volume six of Shin Seinen to use as an example. To increase the interest and plausibility of his drama, he began to carefully practice Shundei's handwriting using this sample. The pencil traces on the original are testimony to this.

After Oyamada had created Hirata's hate mail, he sent the envelopes from different post offices one by one, with a suitable number of days intervening between each. It was not for nothing that he would stop at the nearest post box while motoring about on business. As to the content of the letters, he would have found out about Shundei's past through articles in the newspapers and magazines. The details of Shizuko's activities he could have spied from above the ceiling and what he could not tell from there he would have been able to describe because he was after all her husband. He would have memorized Shizuko's phrasing and gestures from the pillow talk they exchanged when beside each other in bed and put these down on paper to suggest they had been observed by a peeping Shundei. What a fiend! By concealing himself and using someone else's name in the threatening letters, he was able *to experience the crime-tinged frisson of sending the documents to his wife and the devilish pleasure of spying on her from the attic with excitement while she read and shuddered in fear. Furthermore, there is cause to believe that during the intervals he continued with the whip lashings because it was after his death that the scar on the nape of Shizuko's neck first disappeared. While he tortured his wife Shizuko thus, he perpetrated such cruelty precisely because of his idolization of her and not from any sense of hatred. You will of course be well aware of the psychology of this type of sexual deviant.*

*I have completely outlined above the deductive reasoning that leads me to believe Oyamada Rokurō was the one who wrote the threatening letters. Why then did what was only a mischievous prank by a sexual degenerate result in this murder case? Why was it that Oyamada himself was murdered? Not only that, why was he wearing a strange wig and floating naked under Azumabashi bridge? Who was responsible for the stab wounds in his back? If Ōe Shundei was not involved in this case, then a spate of questions arise, including whether there was a different criminal. I must state my observations and deductions concerning this.*

*To put it simply, he may have been punished by heaven, perhaps because the extreme immorality of his devilry evoked divine wrath. There was no crime of any sort, nor any perpetrator – just Oyamada's accidental death. This prompts a question about the fatal wound in his back, but I shall answer that later, for I must follow the course of events in order and explain why I came to think this way.*

*My deductive trail commences with nothing other than his wig. You will perhaps recall that in order to prevent anyone spying on her Shizuko relocated her sleeping quarters to the second floor of the European-style annexe on 17 March, the day after I had searched the attic. While it is not clear to what lengths Shizuko went in explaining the need for this to her husband or why he agreed with her, it would have been from that day that he was no longer able to pry on her from the chink in the ceiling. But if we exert our imagination, we can* envisage that peeping through this opening would have started to become somewhat boring around this time. Perhaps the shifting of their bedroom to the European section of the house fortuitously provided the opportunity for another piece of mischief. The wig helps answer why. The fluffy wig that he himself had ordered. As he had ordered the hair-piece at the end of last year, there must initially have been a different use for it but now the wig was just right for the new situation.

He had seen Shundei's photograph in the frontispiece to 'Games in the Attic.' As this was apparently a likeness of the young Shundei, naturally enough he was not bald like Oyamada but bore a head of fluffy black hair. If Oyamada had progressed from frightening Shizuko through letters and concealment in the shadowy attic, and now schemed to become Ōe Shundei himself (in order to experience the strange sensation of Shizuko noting his presence and exposing his face to her briefly in the window of the European wing of their home), he would surely have had to hide his bald head, which would be the first thing to give away his identity. This was exactly the right sort of wig. If he wore the hair-piece, there would be no concern of the terrified Shizuko making out who it was when he flashed his face on the far side of the dark glass (and this means would be all the more effective).

That night (19 March), the gate was still open when Oyamada returned from playing go with his friend Koume. Accordingly, unnoticed by the servants he quietly rounded the garden and slipped into the study beneath the stairs in the European annexe (Shizuko heard this; he kept that key on the same chain as the key to the book cabinet). There in the darkness he put on the wig, taking care that he did not disturb Shizuko in the bedroom above. He then went out, passed through the trees, climbed on to the eaves moulding and moved around outside the bedroom window where he lifted the blind and peeked in. This must have been the moment Shizuko later recounted when she saw a person's face through the window.

*Before explaining how it was that Oyamada came to die, I must relate the observations I made when I peered out from the window in question on my second visit to the Oyamada household after beginning to suspect him. As you yourself will be able to confirm the details if you look, I shall forgo a minute portrayal. The window faces the Sumida River; there is hardly any empty ground underneath the eaves and this is enclosed by the same concrete wall as in front; quite a steep stone cliff follows directly on the other side. To maximize the land area, the wall stands on the edge of the stone cliff.*

*The upper section of the wall is about four metres above the water's surface and the second-floor window is some two metres from the wall's top. If Oyamada lost his footing on the eaves moulding (which is very narrow) and fell, there is the possibility that he might have the good fortune to fall inside the wall (a cramped space where two people would have difficulty passing each other) but if that was not the case once he hit the wall he would then tumble into the Sumida River. Of course, in Rokurō's case the latter occurred.*

*As soon as I took note of the Sumida River's current, it seemed more natural to me to think that the corpse had drifted downstream from the spot where it had been thrown in rather than remaining there. I was also aware that the European annexe of the Oyamada home was right beside the river and upstream from Inazumabashi bridge. Accordingly, the thought crossed my mind that Oyamada had fallen from near the window, but it puzzled me for a long time that the cause of death was not drowning but the stab wound in his back.*

*Then one day I remembered a true story resembling this case that I had read about in 'The Latest Crime Investigation Methods,' by Nanba Mokusaburō. I remembered the article because I referred to this book when considering my detective fiction. The story is as follows:*

*'Around the middle of May in the sixth year of the Taishō period (1917), the body of a dead man washed ashore in the vicinity of the Taikō Steamship K.K. breakwater in Otsu City, Shiga Prefecture. The corpse's head bore a cut that looked very much as though it had been*

made by a sharp instrument. The investigating physician determined that the wound was received when the man was alive and was the cause of death, while the presence of some water in the abdomen indicated that the body had been thrown into the water at the time of the murder. At this point, we detectives commenced our activities, believing this to be a major case. We exhausted every method we knew to ascertain the victim's identity, but were unable to come up with a lead. The Otsu police station had received a missing persons notification from a Mr Saitō, a goldsmith from Jofukuji-dori, Kamigyō-ku, Kyoto, regarding an employee named Kobayashi Shigezō (23). A few days later, the numerous similarities between the clothing of this subject and the victim in our case led the station to immediately contact Saitō to view the dead body. It became clear that this was indeed the said employee, and also that neither murder nor suicide could be confirmed. It seems that the dead man had used a considerable amount of his employer's money and disappeared leaving a will. The cut to the head resulted when he threw himself into the lake and the revolving screw of a passing steamer left a wound resembling a slash.'

If I had not remembered this true story, I would probably not have come up with such a fantastic-seeming idea. However, in many cases truth is stranger than fiction and that which appears unbelievably outlandish can actually happen with ease. Still, I am not saying that Oyamada was wounded by a ship's propeller. Slightly unlike the story above, in this case no water at all had been swallowed and there are very few steamers plying the Sumida River at one o'clock in the morning.

But what could have caused the wound in Oyamada's back, which was so deep as to reach his lung? What could have made a wound that so resembled that of a blade? Of course, it had to have been the shards of beer bottles embedded on top of the concrete wall around the Oyamada home to ward off thieves. As these are exactly the same as those visible at the building's front gate, you will perhaps have seen them yourself. Some of them are so large they could well cause a wound that *would reach the lungs. Given that Oyamada struck these at some speed as he fell from the eaves moulding, it is hardly surprising he sustained such an awful wound. Moreover, this interpretation explains the numerous shallow stab marks around the fatal wound.*

*Thus, as befit his vice, Oyamada lost his footing on the roof and received a fatal wound when he struck the wall before falling into the upper Sumida River. Flowing with the current, he floated under the toilet at the Azumabashi steamer landing place in an ignominious death he brought on himself. I have stated above most of my new interpretation related to this case. One or two points remain for me to explain. As to why Rokurō's corpse was naked, the extremity of Azumabashi bridge is the haunt of vagrants, beggars, and persons with criminal records and if the drowned man's body wore expensive garments (that night Rokurō wore an Ōshima kimono, a haori, and a platinum pocket watch), I think it is sufficient to point out that there would be numerous villains who would steal these late at night out of sight (NB: my speculation proved to be true, for a vagrant was indeed arrested later). Next, reasons you may consider that would explain why Shizuko did not hear Rokurō fall even though she was in the bedroom include that she was out of her wits with fear at that moment; the glass window in the concrete European annexe was tightly closed; there is a considerable distance from the window to the water's surface; and even if the splash were audible, it may have been drowned out by the sound of oars and paddles from the mud carriers that sometimes pass along the Sumida River through the night. I think it should be noted that there is not even a hint of foul play in this case and while it led to an unfortunate and bizarre death there was absolutely nothing that went beyond the bounds of a prank. Otherwise, there is no explaining the complete lack of attention to detail by Oyamada, who gave his gloves – a piece of evidence – to the driver, used his real name when ordering the wig, and left crucial pieces of evidence in the book cabinet in his home, albeit under lock and key . . .*

I have reproduced my statement at great length, but I inserted it here because if I do not make my deductions clear, what I am to write now would be very difficult to understand.

I noted in this statement that Ōe Shundei was not a presence from the very first. But was this actually the case? If so, the extensive details provided about him in the first chapter of my record would have been completely pointless.

10

The date on the personal account written for submission to Inspector Itosaki is 28 April. First, though, I visited the Oyamada home the day after writing the document to show it to Shizuko and calm her down by informing her that there was now no need to fear the Ōe Shundei phantasm. Since coming to suspect Oyamada, I had visited twice to conduct a sort of house search, but I had not yet told her about this.

At that time, relatives were gathering around Shizuko in connection with the disposal of Oyamada's estate, and it seemed that a number of troublesome issues had arisen, but in her isolated state Shizuko relied on me to a considerable extent, making a great fuss in welcoming me when I visited. After passing through as usual to Shizuko's parlour, I surprised her by very abruptly saying 'Shizuko, you have nothing to worry about now. There was no Ōe Shundei from the first.' Naturally, she did not understand what I meant. I then read aloud a draft of the personal statement that I had brought with me in much the same manner as I always read my detective fiction to friends after completing a story. For one thing, I wanted to allay Shizuko's concerns by informing her of the details; for another I intended to obtain her opinion and discover any shortcomings in order to thoroughly correct the draft.

The section regarding Oyamada's sadistic perversion was very cruel. Shizuko's face reddened and it seemed as though she would like to disappear. In the part touching on the gloves, she commented, 'I thought it strange because I was certain there was one more.'

At the place regarding Rokurō's death by misadventure, she was so shocked that she turned pale and it seemed she was unable to speak.

A little while after I had finished reading she said 'Oh!' remaining blank until eventually a slight expression of relief appeared on her face. When she knew that the threatening letters from Ōe Shundei were not real and that she was no longer in any danger, she must surely have felt a great sense of relief.

If my selfish suspicions may be allowed, I believe that she must certainly have experienced some easing of guilt regarding her illicit relationship with me when she heard about the terrible harvest that Oyamada had reaped.

She would have actually been pleased to have reached a situation in which she could excuse herself, saying 'Oh my, to think that he made me suffer by committing such horrible acts . . .'

As for myself, I was pleased that she had acknowledged the truth of my statement and I unwittingly drank too much at her bidding. Not being a strong drinker, I soon turned red and then, much unlike my normal self, melancholy. I sat there without saying anything, gazing at Shizuko's face.

Shizuko looked quite careworn, but that paleness was her natural colour and that strange attraction reflecting the powerful elasticity of her overall body and the dark flame burning within her core had not only not dwindled in the least, as we were now in the season for woollen garments, the contour of her form appeared more voluptuous than ever dressed in an old-style flannel. Set aquiver by that garment, I gazed at the writhing curves of her limbs and though it troubled me I limned in my heart the parts of her body swathed in some as yet unknown material.

After we had talked together for a while, I came up with a marvellous plan under the influence of the alcohol. I would rent a house in an out of the way spot to be used for assignations between Shizuko and myself and the two of us would enjoy our secret trysts without anyone knowing.

I must make the miserable confession that after making sure that the maid had left I then drew Shizuko suddenly to me and we kissed for the second time. I put both hands behind her back, enjoying the feel of the flannel while I whispered my idea in her ear. She did not rebuff my impolite advances and even accepted my suggestion with a slight nod.

How shall I describe the dreamlike sequence of trysts we enjoyed frequently over the next twenty days or so?

I rented an old house with a mud-walled storehouse on the riverbank near the famous Ogyō-no-Matsu pine tree in Negishi. I asked an old lady from the neighbourhood corner store to look after it and Shizuko usually arranged to meet here during the day.

For the first time in my life, I tasted keenly the intensity and power of a woman's passion. Sometimes, we were like little children, me with my tongue out panting near her shoulder like a hunting hound as we rushed together around the building, which was as big as an old haunted house. As I reached out to catch her, she would twist her body skilfully like a dolphin, evading my grasp and running away. We ran until, almost dead with exhaustion and out of breath, we collapsed together in a tangle.

At other times, we shut ourselves up for one or two hours in the silence of the dark earthen storehouse. Someone listening intently at the entrance would have heard from within the sound of a woman sobbing sadly mixed in, as in a harmony, with the deep sound of a man crying unrestrainedly.

But one day, I became afraid when Shizuko brought the

riding whip, used regularly by Oyamada, hidden in a large bunch of peonies. She pressed the whip into my hand and made me lash her naked flesh as Oyamada had.

Having suffered cruelty at Rokurō's hands for such a long time, the perversion had taken root in her and she was now plagued by the irresistible appetite of a masochist. Had my assignations with her continued this way for half a year, I too would surely have been possessed by the same sickness as Oyamada.

For I shuddered to note the odd joy I felt when, unable to refuse Shizuko's request, I applied the whip to her delicate body and saw the poisonous-looking weals rise instantly on the surface of her pale skin.

However, I did not start this record in order to outline the love affair between a man and a woman. As I intend to describe this in more detail another day when I use it to create a piece of fiction, I shall here only note one fact heard from Shizuko during the days of passion we passed together.

This was in connection with Rokurō's wig. Actually, Rokurō had gone to the trouble of ordering this and having it made to hide his unattractive baldness in bedroom romps with Shizuko and although she had laughed about it and sought to stop him, such was his considerable sensitivity on these matters that he went off to place the order as serious as a child. When I asked Shizuko why she had hidden this, she answered 'I couldn't talk about that – it's embarrassing.'

About twenty days had passed by and as I thought it might seem strange if I was not seen at the Oyamada home I pretended nothing untoward had happened and visited the house, meeting with Shizuko and conversing very formally with her for about an hour, after which she saw me to the hallway and I went home by taxi. By coincidence, the driver was Aoki Tamizou, the man from whom I had earlier purchased the gloves, and this proved to be the event that saw me drawn into a bizarre daylight dream.

The gloves were different, but there was no change at all from about a month ago in the shape of the hands gripping the steering wheel, the old-fashioned dark-blue spring overcoat (which he wore directly over his collared shirt), the appearance of those bulky shoulders, the windscreen, and the mirror above, and that induced in me a sense of uneasiness.

I remembered that I had addressed the driver as Ōe Shundei. Then I found that I was thinking solely of Ōe Shundei – the face in the photograph, the bizarre plots of his stories, recollections of his peculiar daily existence. Finally, I felt his presence so keenly that it seemed as if he were sitting on the cushion right beside me. My mind was a blank and in an instant I blurted out, 'You there, Aoki. You know those gloves: when was it that Mr Oyamada gave them to you?'

'What?' the driver replied turning to me with a bewildered expression, just as he had a month earlier. 'Well, it was last year of course, in November . . . I'm sure it was on the day I received my monthly salary from accounts because I remember thinking well I'm getting lots of things today. That makes it the 28th of November. I'm certain of it.'

'The 28th of November, you say?'

With my mind still blank, I simply repeated the driver's reply.

'Why are you so preoccupied with the gloves, sir? Was there something special about them?'

The driver was leering, but I said nothing and stared intently at a speck of dust on the windscreen. I remained that way while the car travelled for four or five blocks. Suddenly, I rose up inside the vehicle, grabbed the driver's shoulder, and shouted, 'You're sure it was the 28th of November? Would you be prepared to swear to it in court?'

The taxi had swerved and the driver was adjusting the

steering wheel to bring the car under control. 'In a court? Is this some sort of joke? But I'm certain it was the 28th of November. I've even got a witness. My relief driver saw them too.'

Although Aoki was very surprised, he could see how serious I was and he replied earnestly.

'Right then, take me back now.'

Although he was growing more confused and looked a little afraid, the driver turned the taxi around as I had asked and took me to the front gate of the Oyamada home. I leaped out and rushed to the entrance. Taking hold of the maid who happened to be there, I demanded, 'In the major house cleaning at the end of last year the boards of the ceiling in the Japanese section of the house were apparently completely stripped and washed. Is that true?'

I knew this because, as I have indicated above, Shizuko told me when I went up into the attic. The maid must have thought me mad. For a while she looked at me intently before saying, 'Yes, that is true, sir. It wasn't a full scale washing – just cleaning down with water – but the house cleaners were certainly here. It was the 25th of December.'

'The ceilings of all the rooms?'

'Yes, the ceiling of every room.'

Perhaps having heard all this, Shizuko emerged from the house and asked me with a worried look, 'What has happened?'

I repeated my question and after Shizuko had given the same reply as the maid I said a quick goodbye, flew into the taxi, ordered the driver to take me to my lodgings, and sank deep into the cushions and the muddy fantasy that seemed to have taken hold of me.

The boards in the ceiling of the Japanese section of the Oyamada home had been taken up and washed with water last year on the 25th of December. Thus, the ornamental button had to have fallen in the attic after that.

However, the gloves had been given to the taxi driver on the

28th of November. As I have noted above several times, there is no doubting the fact that the ornamental button had fallen from those gloves.

Accordingly, the button from the gloves in question had been lost in a place in which it could not have fallen. I realized what it was this puzzling phenomenon indicated.

In order to be certain, I visited Aoki Tamizou at his garage and met the assistant driver, who confirmed that it had indeed been the 28th of November. I also visited the contractors who had cleaned the ceiling of the Oyamada household and learned that the 25th of December was the correct date. They assured me that nothing, no matter how small the object, could have been left there.

The only explanation that would enable the claim that Oyamada had dropped that button to be maintained is as follows.

The button remained in Oyamada's pocket after it fell from the glove. Unaware of this and not wanting to use a buttonless glove, Oyamada gave them to the driver. In a strange turn of events, the button accidentally fell from Oyamada's pocket when he subsequently climbed into the attic anywhere from a month, at the earliest, to three months later (the threatening letters first began to arrive in February).

It seems strange that the button was in the pocket of Oyamada's waistcoat rather than an overcoat (usually gloves end up in overcoat pockets and it is unthinkable that Oyamada would have worn an overcoat when he climbed up into the attic; indeed, it would even be somewhat unnatural for him to have worn a jacket when he entered the space) and surely a man of means such as Oyamada would not have worn his winter clothes through the spring.

As a result, the pall of darkness cast by Ōe Shundei, the beast in the shadows, spread ever further over my soul.

The news that Oyamada was a sexual fiend such as might be

found in a modern detective story had perhaps triggered in me a monumental delusion (though the fact that he had lashed Shizuko with a riding whip was beyond doubt). It might be that he was killed for somebody's purpose.

Ōe Shundei! Ah the image of that beast persists tenaciously within my soul.

Strange, how once the thought begins to bud, everything comes to seem suspicious. That a mere fiction writer like myself should have been able to make the deductions in that personal statement with such ease also seems odd when you think about it. Actually, I had left the draft of the statement uncorrected because I thought an outrageous mistake could be concealed in it somewhere and partly too because I was so absorbed in my affair with Shizuko. The fact is that somehow I did not want to go ahead with it and indeed I had actually come to think that was for the best.

Thinking about it, there is too much evidence on hand in this case. At every turn I made, pieces of evidence rolled about all too conveniently, as if they were lying in wait. Just as Ōe Shundei himself says in his works, detectives must exercise caution when they encounter too much proof.

First, it is hard to believe that Oyamada had forged the genuine-looking lettering of the threatening letters, as I had imagined. As Honda had said, even if it were possible to write characters that resembled Shundei's handwriting, how could anyone copy his unique style, particularly an entrepreneur like Oyamada from a different field?

Only now did I remember a story written by Shundei called 'The Stamp' about a mentally unbalanced medical doctor's wife who hates her husband. She learns how to write like him and forges a document in his hand as part of a scheme to make the doctor appear guilty of murder. Perhaps Shundei had done the same thing to bring about Oyamada's downfall.

Depending on your viewpoint, this case seemed just like a collection of Ōe Shundei's masterpieces. The peeping from behind the ceiling boards was from 'Games in the Attic' and the piece of evidence in the form of a button was also an idea taken from this work. The forging of Shundei's hand came from 'The Stamp', while the raw wound on the nape of Shizuko's neck hinting at a sadist emulated the approach used in 'Murder on "B" Hill.' Indeed the whole case smacked strongly of Ōe Shundei, including the glass shard that had caused the stab wound and the naked body floating under the toilet.

There seemed to be too many odd coincidences. It was as if Shundei had overshadowed the case from start to finish. I felt that I had followed Ōe Shundei's instructions in piecing together deductions exactly as he wished. It even seemed that I had been possessed by Shundei.

Shundei was here somewhere. I was certain that serpent-like eyes glittered at the bottom of this case. It was not my mind theorizing – I sensed it within myself. He had to be here somewhere.

I was thinking about this as I lay on my futon in a room at my lodgings. Strong as my constitution was, even I was now tired of this never-ending fantasy. Thinking it over and over, I finally nodded off with fatigue. I awoke from a strange dream with a start and an odd idea came into my head.

It was late at night, but I called Honda's lodgings and asked for him.

When he answered the telephone, I surprised him by asking without any preliminaries, 'Now, you told me that Ōe Shundei's wife had a round face didn't you?'

After realizing it was me, Honda answered in a sleepy voice.

'Mmn, yes, that's right.'

'She always had her hair done in a European style.'

'Mmn, yes, that's right.'

'She wore spectacles for near sightedness?'

'Yes, that's correct.'

'She had a gold tooth.'

'Yes, that's correct.'

'She had bad teeth, right. And apparently she often applied a poultice to her cheek to kill the tooth pain, didn't she?'

'You are well informed. Have you met Shundei's wife?'

'No. I talked to some of her neighbours in Sakuragi-chō. But she would have been wearing the pain-killing poultice when you met her, right?'

'Yes, she always wore one. I suppose her teeth must have been very bad.'

'Was it the right cheek?'

'I don't remember well, but I have a feeling it was the right.'

'But it seems a little strange that a young woman who wore her hair in the European style would use an old-fashioned poultice for quelling tooth pain. People don't use them nowadays, do they?'

'You're right. But what on earth's this all about? Have you found some clue in the case?'

'I have indeed. I'll tell you all about it later.'

In order to be certain, I thus sought Honda's confirmation of things that I had heard before.

Next, I went to the desk and much as if solving some geometry problem I inscribed on a sheet of paper a variety of shapes and equations, writing and erasing, writing and erasing until it was almost dawn.

II

Now, it was always me who sent the letters arranging our trysts and after three days had passed without contact from me it seemed that Shizuko could wait no longer, for she sent a message by express mail asking me to come to 'our hiding place' tomorrow around three in the afternoon without fail. She also complained, 'Perhaps you no longer like me now that you have discovered my excessively sensual nature. Could it be that you are afraid of me?'

Even after receiving this letter, I did not feel particularly enthusiastic. I just did not want to see her face. Nevertheless, I went to that ghostly house near the Ogyō-no-Matsu pine tree at the time she set.

It was a maddeningly humid day in June, just ahead of the rainy season, and the sky hung down oppressively overhead as gloomy as a cataract. After getting off the train and walking three or four blocks, my armpits and back were clammy with sweat and when I touched my collared shirt it was soaking wet.

Shizuko had arrived a little earlier and was sitting on the bed in the cool storehouse, waiting. We had laid a carpet on the second floor of this building, decorating the scene of our games as effectively as possible with a bed, a sofa, and some large mirrors. Ignoring my pleas to desist, Shizuko had without reserve purchased ridiculously expensive objects, including the sofa and the bed.

She wore a bright single-layer Yukitsumugi kimono and a black silk sash embroidered with fallen paulownia leaves. As usual, her hair was done in a shiny *marumage* bob and she lounged on the bed's pure white sheets. But the harmony of the European furnishings and her traditional Edo style contrasted bizarrely in the storehouse's dark second storey. Although now a widow, Shizuko continued to wear her hair in a style denoting a married woman, and when I saw that scented, shining *marumage* bob of which she was so fond, I immediately beheld her in a lascivious light, the *marumage* falling apart, the front locks dishevelled, and straggling wisps in a tangle at her neck. For she usually spent as much as thirty minutes in front of the mirror combing her tousled hair before leaving the house we used for our assignations.

As soon as I came in, Shizuko asked me, 'Why did you come back the other day just to ask about the house cleaning? You seemed very agitated. I wondered what it could be, but I couldn't think what it was.'

Taking off my coat I said, 'You couldn't think what it was? Something very important. I made a big mistake. The attic was cleaned at the end of December and the button fell off Oyamada's glove over a month before that. You see, he gave the gloves to the taxi driver on the 28th of November, so the button must have come off before that. The order is all topsy turvy.'

'My!' said Shizuko with a startled look, but it seemed she had not fully grasped the situation for she went on 'But the button fell in the attic after it had come off the glove then.'

'Well, it was after, but the issue here is how long after. It would be strange if the button did not fall when Oyamada climbed into the attic. Precisely speaking, the button fell after, but it fell in the attic at that same time and was left there. You'll agree that it would be beyond the laws of physics to think that the button took more than a month to fall after it had been torn off?'

'I suppose so,' said Shizuko, who had grown somewhat pale and was still thinking.

'If the button was in Oyamada's pocket after dropping off and then accidentally fell in the attic a month later, that would make sense, but do you think Oyamada would have worn the clothes he used in November last year through this spring?'

'No. He was very fastidious about his appearance and at the end of the year he changed over completely to thick, warm clothing.'

'You see. That's why it's strange.'

'Well,' she said, drawing a breath, 'then surely Hirata . . .'

'Of course. This case smacks too strongly of Ōe Shundei. I have to completely amend that statement I wrote recently.'

I then explained to her in a simple fashion that, as noted in the preceding chapter, this case resembled a collection of Ōe Shundei's masterpieces, that there was too much evidence, and the forging of handwriting seemed all too genuine.

'You won't be well aware of it, but Shundei has a truly strange lifestyle. Why didn't he receive guests? Why did he seek to avoid visitors by shifting house so often, going on trips, and falling ill? Finally, why did he waste money by continuing to pay rent on that empty house in Mukōjima Susaki-chō? Even for a misanthropic novelist, that seems very odd. Too odd, don't you think, unless it was in preparation for murdering someone?'

I was sitting beside Shizuko on the bed as I spoke. When she thought that it could after all be Shundei's handiwork, she quickly became frightened, slid her body right against me, and gripped my left wrist with a clammy hand.

'Now I realize what a fool he made of me, how I did exactly as he wanted. I was put through my paces too with all that false evidence he had set up beforehand, following his deductions directly as a guide. Ha, ha, ha . . .'

I laughed in self-mockery.

'He's an awful creature. He grasped my way of thinking exactly and set up the evidence accordingly. Why, an ordinary sleuth would have been no good. It had to be a novelist like me with a penchant for deduction because no-one else would have had such a roundabout and bizarre imagination. However, if Shundei is the criminal, a number of illogical points arise. Still, arise though they may, it is because the case is so hard to solve and Shundei such an unfathomable villain.

'When you boil it all down, there are two such points. The first is that the threatening letters suddenly ceased to arrive after Oyamada's death. The second is why the diaries, Shundei's book, and *Shin Seinen* came to be in Oyamada's book cabinet.

'If Shundei really is the criminal, these two points just do not add up. If he copied Oyamada's hand and wrote in the margins of the diaries and made the traces of writing found in the frontispiece of *Shin Seinen* in order to put together "evidence," the thing that is really hard to understand is how Shundei could have obtained the key to the book cabinet because this was carried by Oyamada alone. Next, did he sneak into Oyamada's study?

'I have been thinking about these points so much over the past three days that my head hurts. In the end, I managed to come up with what I think may be the only explanation.

'Given the pervading stench of Shundei's works in this case, I took out his stories and began to read them, thinking that a closer study of his fiction might provide some key to solve this case. Although I have not told you yet, Shundei had apparently been wandering around Asakusa Park in strange garb, including a clown's costume and pointed hat, according to an expert in these matters called Honda. When I inquired about this at some advertising agencies, they could only think that it must have been a vagrant from the park. That Shundei mingled with the homeless in Asakusa Park seems like something right out of Stevenson's *The Strange Case of Dr Jekyll and Mr Hyde*, don't you think? After realizing this, I searched for something similar in Shundei's fiction and discovered two pieces that you will perhaps know: "Panorama Country," a long story published immediately before he went missing, and "One Person, Two Roles," a short story published earlier. When I read these, I understood well how attracted he was by a Dr Jekyll-type approach, in which one person could transform into two.'

'You're scaring me,' said Shizuko, gripping my hand tightly.

'The way you're speaking is strange. Let's not talk about it, shall we. I don't like it, not here in this dark storeroom. We'll talk about it later. Today let's have fun. When I'm here with you like this, I don't even think about Hirata.'

'Now, listen to me. This has to do with your life. If Shundei still has you in his sights . . .'

I was not in the mood for lovers' games.

'I have still only found two odd correspondences in this case. At the risk of sounding like an academic, one is spatial and the other temporal. Now, here is a map of Tokyo.'

I took out of my pocket a simple map of Tokyo that I had prepared and pointed with my finger as I talked.

'I recall from my conversations with Honda, and the head of the Kisagata police station, the various addresses that Ōe Shundei flitted to one after the other. As I remember, there was Ikebukuro, Kikui, Negishi, Hatsune, Kanasugi, Suehiro, Sakuragi, Yanagi-shima, and Susaki. Ikebukuro and Kikui are very distant, but if you look at the map you'll see the other seven places are concentrated in a narrow area in the north-east corner. This was a major oversight on Shundei's part. The significance of Ikebukuro and Kikui being so far apart is easy to understand if you consider that it was from the time Shundei lived in Negishi that his literary fame grew and visitors began to throng to his home. Up until the Kikui period, he was able to carry out everything to do with his manuscripts by letter alone. Now, if we trace a line like this from Negishi through the following six places, an irregular circle emerges, and if we were to calculate the centre of that circle we would discover a clue to this case. I will now explain to you exactly what I mean.'

I am not sure what Shizuko was thinking, but letting go of my hand she suddenly put both hands around my neck, smiled that Mona Lisa smile that revealed her eye teeth, and exclaimed 'I'm scared.' Next, she pressed her cheek against my cheek and then her lips against my lips. After a while like that, her lips left mine and next she began to tickle my ear skilfully with her forefinger as she drew closer to my lobe and whispered rhythmically much as if sweetly singing a lullaby.

'I'm so disappointed that we have lost precious time with this frightening talk. My darling, can you not feel the fire burning within my lips? Don't you hear the drumming within my breast? Hold me, my dear. Hold me.'

But I continued speaking regardless, 'Just a little longer. There's not much more. Just bear with me and hear me out. I came here today because I really wanted to discuss things with you. Now, as to the temporal correspondence. I remember well that Shundei's name suddenly disappeared from the magazines at the end of last year. You say that it was also at the end of last year that Oyamada came back from overseas, right? I ask myself why these two things coincide so neatly. Is it just coincidence? What do you think?'

Before I had finished speaking, Shizuko brought the riding whip from the corner of the room, pressed it into my right hand, stripped off her clothes, and fell forward on to the bed. Only her face looked back at me from under the smooth naked shoulder.

'What of it? What of it?' she babbled wildly. 'Now, whip me! Whip me!' she screamed, moving the upper half of her body like a wave.

A mouse-coloured sky showed through the storehouse's small window. My head thrummed as something like distant thunder, perhaps the sound of a train, mixed in with the ringing in my ears. I grew uneasy when I thought that it also sounded like the drumming of an evil army marching down from the sky. Perhaps it was the weather and the peculiar atmosphere inside the storeroom that made us both mad. Looking back on it, I realize that we were not of sound mind. Gazing down on her pale, sweaty body writhing on its side, I continued tenaciously with my reasoning.

'On the one hand, it is as clear as day that Ōe Shundei is involved in this case. But on the other hand, the might of Japan's constabulary has been unable to ascertain the whereabouts of a famous novelist after two full months and it seems that he has vanished without a trace.

'It terrifies me even to think of it. The strange part is that this is not a nightmare. Why does he not attempt to kill Oyamada Shizuko? He has suddenly stopped writing those threatening letters. What ninja technique did he use to sneak into Oyamada's study? And then he was able to open that locked book cabinet . . .

'I could not help but recall a certain person – Hirayama Hideko, the female detective fiction author. Everyone thinks the author is a woman, including many writers and journalists. Apparently love letters arrive daily at Hideko's house from admiring readers. But the truth is Hideko is a man. In fact, he is an established government official.

'All writers of detective fiction are peculiar, including Shundei, Hirayama Hideko, and myself. That is what happens when a man pretends to be a woman and bizarre tastes gather force. One author used to dress up as a woman and hang around Asakusa at night. He even played at being in love with another man.'

I continued to babble crazily as if in a trance. My face was covered in sweat that coursed unpleasantly into my mouth.

'Alright Shizuko. Listen closely. Is there some fault in my reasoning? Where is the centre of the circle traced by Shundei's addresses? Please look at the map. It is your house: Yama no Shuku, in Asakusa. All the addresses are within ten minutes of your home.

'Why did Shundei go into hiding at the same time your husband died? It's because you have stopped attending tea-ceremony and music classes. Do you understand? While Oyamada was away, you used to attend tea-ceremony and music classes every day from the afternoon into the evening.

'Who was it that set things up perfectly and led me to make my conclusions? It was you! It was you who lay in wait for me at the museum and thereafter manipulated me at your will.

'You would easily have been able to add the little phrases to the diaries and put the other evidence in Oyamada's book cabinet as well as to drop the button in the attic. This is what I have been able to deduce. Is there any other way to think about it? Now, what do you say? Please answer me.'

Crying out, 'I can't bear this. It's too much!' the naked Shizuko clung to me. She pressed her cheek against my collared shirt and began to cry so hard that I could feel the warm tears on my skin.

'Why do you cry? Why have you been trying to stop me from proceeding with my deductions? Surely you would want to hear me if it were a matter of life or death for you. That alone makes me suspect you. Listen to me. I have not finished yet.

'Why did Ōe Shundei's wife wear glasses? Why the gold teeth and the poultice for tooth pain? And the Western hairstyle and round face? Is that not exactly the same disguise used in "Panorama Country"? In this story Shundei describes the essentials for disguising a Japanese person's appearance – altering the hairstyle, wearing spectacles, plumping out contours – and in "The Copper Penny" he writes about covering a healthy tooth with a gold-plated outer bought from a gewgaw stall.

'You have easily recognizable eye teeth. To hide them, you wore gold-plated outer covers. You have a large mole on your right cheek and to disguise that you applied the poultice. And it would be easy to make your oval face look rounder by doing your hair in a Western style. This is how you transformed yourself into Shundei's wife.

'Yesterday I let Honda catch a glimpse of you to confirm with him whether you resembled Shundei's wife. What do you know – he said you would look exactly like her if your *marumage* was changed to a Western hairstyle and you wore glasses and gold teeth. Come on now, let's have it all out. I have grasped everything completely. Do you intend to keep deceiving me?'

I shook Shizuko off. She fell heavily on the bed, burst into tears, and would not answer no matter how long I waited. I was quite agitated and without thinking I raised the riding whip and lashed her naked back. *Take that, and that,* I thought as, losing control, I lashed and lashed. Gradually the redness spread on her pale skin until a wormlike wound stained with scarlet blood took shape. She lay there at my feet in the same lewd pose as always, with her hands and feet writhing and her body undulating. Then, in the final light breath of one about to faint, she whispered in a small voice 'Hirata, Hirata.'

'Hirata? So you are still trying to deceive me? If you transformed yourself into Shundei's wife, would you have me believe that a separate person called Shundei actually exists? You know he does not. He is a fictional character. To cover that up, you pretended to be his wife and met the magazine journalists and everyone else. And you changed addresses so many times. But as there were some people who would not be convinced by a completely imaginary character, you hired a vagrant from Asakusa Park and had him sleep in that room. It is not that Shundei transformed himself into the man in the clown's outfit – the man in the clown's outfit transformed himself into Shundei.'

Shizuko remained silent as death on the bed. Only the livid wound on her back writhed as if alive as she breathed. She remained quiet and my agitation gradually abated.

'Shizuko, I did not mean to do such a terrible thing to you. I should have spoken more quietly, but you tried so hard to avoid listening to what I had to say and you sought to cover up with such coquettish behaviour that I am afraid I lost control. Please forgive me. Now, it's alright for you not to say anything because I will try to outline everything you did in order. If I make a mistake, be sure to say something and let me know, won't you?'

Then I explained my reasoning in a way that would be easy to understand.

'You are blessed with uncommon sagacity and literary talent for a woman. I saw that very clearly just from reading the letters you wrote. It was entirely plausible that you should have wanted to write detective fiction under a nom de plume, and a man's name at that. However, your stories were exceptionally well received. Then, at exactly the same time as your name started to become famous, Oyamada went overseas for two years. To ease your loneliness and to satisfy your bizarre proclivities you came up with the fearful trick of one person playing three roles. You wrote a novel called 'One Person, Two Roles,' but you went one step further and conceived of one person playing three roles.

'You rented a house in Negishi under the name of Hirata Ichirō. The earlier addresses in Ikebukuro and Kikui were only set up for receiving mail. Inventing "misanthropy" and "trips" to hide Hirata from view, you used disguise to transform yourself into his wife and completely took over as his agent in discussions related to his drafts. Thus, when these were being written, you became Hirata–Ōe Shundei and met the magazine journalists; when renting a house, you became Mrs Hirata; and at the Oyamada household in Yama no Shuku, you were Mrs Oyamada. In this way then, one person played three roles.

'For that reason, you needed to be away from the house and so nearly every day you would go out for the whole afternoon saying that you were off to practise the tea ceremony or music. The one body was used to play Mrs Oyamada for half the day and Mrs Hirata for the other half. Somewhere far away would not do because you needed time to disguise yourself by arranging your hair and changing your clothes. Accordingly, when you changed addresses you selected a location about ten minutes by car in a radius centred on Yama no Shuku.

'As I am also a student of the bizarre, I understand your feeling well. For while this was a very burdensome labour, there could hardly be another game in this world as amusing as this.

'I recall now that a critic reviewing Shundei's works once said that they are full to an almost unpleasant degree with suspicion that only a woman could possess. As I remember, the critic said it was much as if a beast in the shadows were writhing in the darkness. That critic was telling the truth, don't you think?

'Two years passed quickly and Oyamada came home. You were no longer able to play three roles. Accordingly, Ōe Shundei then disappeared and there were no particular suspicions because everyone knew of Shundei's extreme aversion to the company of other people.

'But why did you decide to commit that awful crime? As a man, I cannot understand well what you felt, but texts on the psychology of perversion indicate that women with a tendency to hysteria often send threatening letters to themselves. There are numerous cases of this both in Japan and overseas.

'There is a desire to attract pity from others even by scaring oneself. I am sure this is your case.

'Receiving threatening letters from a famous male novelist who is actually you – what a wonderful idea!

'At the same time, you began to feel dissatisfied with your aging husband. You clung to the hard to relinquish desires that you had experienced in that life of perverted freedom. Or it might be closer to the mark to say that for a long time crime and murder had held an inexpressible attraction for you, just as in Shundei's stories. And then there is Shundei, the fictional personage who disappears without a trace. By casting suspicion on him you can be safe forever and in addition you rid yourself of an unpleasant husband and inherit a vast legacy that will enable you to live out the rest of your life as you please.

'But that was not enough to satisfy you. To be completely safe, you decided to put in place a double line of defence. And I was the person you chose. I was always criticizing Shundei's works, so you decided to control me like a puppet in order to wreak your revenge. You must have been highly amused when I showed you my personal statement. Deceiving me was no trouble at all, was it? All it took was the ornamental glove button, the diaries, *Shin Seinen*, and "Games in the Attic."

'But as you note in your novels, criminals always make some silly little mistake. You picked up the button from Oyamada's glove and used it as a vital piece of evidence, but you did not find out when it had fallen off. You had no idea that the gloves had been given to the taxi driver a long time before. What a silly little slip. As to Oyamada's fatal wound, I think it was as I earlier reasoned – with one difference. Oyamada was not peeping through the window. You pushed him out of the window, perhaps in the midst of some amorous romp (which is why he was wearing that wig).

'Alright Shizuko, were there any faults in my deduction? Please answer something. See if you can pick a hole in my reasoning. Come on then Shizuko.'

Shizuko was quite inert, so I placed my hand on her shoulder and shook her gently. Whether shame and remorse prevented her from looking up I do not know, but she did not move or say anything.

Having said everything I wanted to say, I stood there in a disappointed daze. The woman who had been my matchless love until yesterday was now collapsed in front of me fully exposed as the pernicious beast in the shadows. Gazing fixedly at her, at some point my eyes began to burn.

'Well I am leaving now,' I said, coming back to my senses. 'Think about it carefully later and please choose the correct course. Thanks to you, I have over the past month been able to glimpse a world of amorous foolishness that I have never experienced before. Even now, I find it hard to leave you when I think of it. But my good conscience will not allow me to continue my relationship with you like this. Goodbye.'

I left a heartfelt kiss on the weal on Shizuko's back and shortly after I left the ghostly house that had been the scene of our passionate romps. It seemed as if the sky was even lower and that the temperature had climbed further. Although my body was drenched in an unpleasant sweat, my teeth chattered as I wandered along as if I had lost my wits.

I learned that Shizuko had committed suicide in the evening of the following day.

She drowned herself in the Sumida River, perhaps by leaping from the second storey of the Western section of the home, just like Oyamada Rokurō. How awful a thing is fate. A passenger found her body floating by that steamer landing under Azuma-bashi bridge, presumably because it followed the river's current.

A newspaper journalist who knew nothing about it all added at the end of his article, 'Perhaps Mrs Oyamada came to her awful end at the hands of the same criminal who killed Oyam-ada Rokurō.'

Reading this article, I felt profoundly sad thinking of the piti-ful death of my former lover, but then Shizuko's death seemed to me an entirely natural outcome for it was indeed appropriate that she should confess her terrible crime. I believed this for about a month.

However, finally the intensity of my imaginings began to gradually subside and as it did an awful doubt entered my head.

I had not heard Shizuko herself utter a single word of confes-sion. Even though all the evidence was lined up, the interpretation of this evidence was all of my construction. There was no immovable certainty such as in the equation 'two plus two equals four.' Once I had put together my flimsy deductions based solely on the word of the taxi driver and the evidence from the house cleaner, did I not interpret the evidence in a way that was opposite to the truth? I could not deny that the same things could be accounted for by another piece of deductive reasoning.

The truth is that when I challenged Shizuko in the storehouse's second floor, I had at first no intention of going that far. I intended to quietly state my reasons and listen to her defence. But half way through, something in her attitude led me into wicked conjecture and all of a sudden I was making assertions in such an unpleasant way. Finally, even though I tried to make sure several times, she kept her silence and I convinced myself that this proved her guilt. Was this simply me convincing myself?

Certainly, Shizuko committed suicide. (Though was it really suicide? Was she murdered? If so, who was the killer? How terrifying!) But even if she killed herself, does that prove her guilt? There may have been another reason. Perhaps the unforgiving heart of a woman led her to suddenly perceive the vanity of life when I challenged her with my suspicions in that way and she realized there was no means of justifying herself to this person whom she thought she could rely on.

If so, I was clearly her murderer, even if I did not directly lay a hand on her. I mentioned the possibility of murder above, and what else could this be?

Nevertheless, if I am only to be suspected for the death of one woman, I can endure it. But this unfortunate proclivity of mine to fantasy suggests a much more horrifying thought.

Clearly, she loved me. You must consider the feelings of a woman who is doubted by the one she loves and accused of being a fiendish criminal. Did she decide to kill herself precisely because she loved me and was saddened by the persistent suspicions of her lover?

This would apply even if my fearful deductions were correct.

Why then did she decide to murder her husband of so many years? Would the thought of liberty or the inheritance have the power to turn a woman into a murderer? Surely it was love. And surely I was the object of her love.

Ah! Such terrifying suspicions. What should I do? Whether she was a murderer or not, I killed this pitiful woman who loved me so much. I could not escape from my accursed petty moralizing. Is there anything in this world as powerful and beautiful as love? Perhaps I had utterly destroyed this clear, beautiful love with the obstinate heart of a moralist.

However, if as I had imagined she was Ōe Shundei and she perpetrated those terrible crimes, I would still have some peace.

Yet how could I be certain now? Oyamada Rokurō was dead. Oyamada Shizuko was dead. And it seemed as if Ōe Shundei had disappeared forever without trace. Honda had said that Shizuko resembled Shundei's wife, but what sort of proof was 'resemblance'?

I have visited Inspector Itosaki several times to find out about subsequent developments, but as he has only made vague replies there would appear to be no resolution in sight in the search for Ōe Shundei. I asked someone to make inquiries about Hirata Ichirō in Shizuko's hometown and the report came back that Hirata Ichirō had gone missing, for my hope that he was merely a fiction proved vain. But even if a person named Hirata did exist, how could one conclude that he was really Shizuko's former lover, that he was also Ōe Shundei, and that he had killed Oyamada? He was nowhere to be found now and it was not possible to deny that Shizuko could have simply used Hirata as the real name for the character of one of the three roles she played. After gaining the permission of Shizuko's relatives, I thoroughly searched her belongings and documents in order to find some sort of evidence either way, but this move did not achieve any results.

I regret my proclivity to reasoning and fantasy, but regret though I might it is not enough. I feel like walking, searching Japan – no, every corner of the earth – in a lifelong pilgrimage to discover the whereabouts of Hirata Ichirō–Ōe Shundei, even though I know it might be pointless.

But even if I found Shundei perhaps my suffering would only grow, though in different ways depending on whether he was or was not the criminal.

Half a year has passed since Shizuko's tragic death, but Hirata Ichirō has still not appeared and my awful doubts about what now cannot be changed deepen every day.